A sound made Slocum turn his ear to listen. Someone was having a hot firefight with some Apaches.

It must be buffalo soldiers from Fort Huachuca.

They looked like they could use some help. He drew his Colt . . . then raced his horse Red across the flats.

Red was churning up the dry sand, when a buck armed with a Winchester repeater ran out and knelt to take aim. It was in that instant the Apache took to get into position that Slocum sighted on him . . . and rapid-fired three shots. The Apache was hit in the shoulder, his long gun went off into the air, and he sprawled over on his side.

Slocum kicked Red to go faster past the downed buck . . . knowing that in seconds the mounted braves would be hot on his tail. The soldiers shooting at him were his next problem . . .

JAKE LOGAN

SLOCUM

AND

LITTLE BRITCHES

JOVE BOOKS, NEW YORK

THE BERKLEY PUBLISHING GROUP
Published by the Penguin Group
Penguin Group (USA) Inc.
375 Hudson Street, New York, New York 10014, USA
Penguin Group (Canada), 90 Eglinton Avenue East, Suite 700, Toronto, Ontario M4P 2Y3, Canada
(a division of Pearson Penguin Canada Inc.)
Penguin Books Ltd., 80 Strand, London WC2R 0RL, England
Penguin Group Ireland, 25 St. Stephen's Green, Dublin 2, Ireland (a division of Penguin Books Ltd.)
Penguin Group (Australia), 250 Camberwell Road, Camberwell, Victoria 3124, Australia
(a division of Pearson Australia Group Pty. Ltd.)
Penguin Books India Pvt. Ltd., 11 Community Centre, Panchsheel Park, New Delhi—110 017, India
Penguin Group (NZ), 67 Apollo Drive, Rosedale, North Shore 0632, New Zealand
(a division of Pearson New Zealand Ltd.)
Penguin Books (South Africa) (Pty.) Ltd., 24 Sturdee Avenue, Rosebank, Johannesburg 2196,
South Africa

Penguin Books Ltd., Registered Offices: 80 Strand, London WC2R 0RL, England

This is a work of fiction. Names, characters, places, and incidents either are the product of the author's imagination or are used fictitiously, and any resemblance to actual persons, living or dead, business establishments, events, or locales is entirely coincidental.

SLOCUM AND LITTLE BRITCHES

A Jove Book / published by arrangement with the author

PRINTING HISTORY
Jove edition / September 2008

Copyright © 2008 by The Berkley Publishing Group.
Cover illustration by Sergio Giovine.

ISBN: 978-0-515-14521-2

JOVE®
Jove Books are published by The Berkley Publishing Group,
a division of Penguin Group (USA) Inc.
375 Hudson Street, New York, New York 10014.
JOVE is a registered trademark of Penguin Group (USA) Inc.
The "J" design is a trademark belonging to Penguin Group (USA) Inc.

PRINTED IN THE UNITED STATES OF AMERICA

10 9 8 7 6 5 4 3 2 1

1

The bitter smell of hot creosote and alkali burned his nostrils. Beads of sweat ran down his temples, but the spindly greasewood distorted his view through the field binoculars of the pale-skinned hostage with her hands tied to the saddle horn. She was being led away by a brown-bodied Apache with a red headband. The fact that a white woman was the Apache's captive disturbed him even more than the pesky flies or the desert's blazing heat. Through the lenses, he could see the buck was pounding the sides of his pony with his moccasin heels and urging it uphill with the woman in tow.

Who was she? In the distance, she looked like someone of wealth. Half of her clothes were torn off, exposing her bare white shoulders, and her once-fancy blond hair looked in disarray. Slocum sprang to his feet and headed downhill for his horse. If he hurried, he had one way he could possibly save her. The 45×3.5 Remington rolling-block rifle under his left stirrup—his best bet to make the long-distance shot he'd need to bring down her kidnapper.

His boot heels rumbled over the loose gravel on the steep grade down to the wash. He went up to Red, the stout strawberry roan gelding, and drew the carbine out of the scabbard. If the telescopic sight was still aligned, he'd perhaps have one chance to stop the woman's captor. He opened the breech, slipped in the paper cartridge from his saddlebag, closed the block, reset the trigger on safety, and churned his way back up the slope.

There might be more Apaches. This could be the most foolish thing he'd ever tried—but he had to attempt to save the woman regardless of the outcome. On his belly again, he took aim. If the buck stayed his course, he would emerge one more time near the crest of that far hill before he was absorbed into Apacheria. Slocum looked through the scope and could see the branches of some lacy mesquite. Trigger cocked, he heard the Apache shouting at the horses in the distance, and finally, through the scope, he could see the renegade's outstretched arm leading the woman's reluctant pony.

He drew in his breath and held it. His right eye bore down on the crosshairs set on the Apache's brown shoulder blades. Then Slocum's curled finger closed on the trigger. The recoil hit his shoulder like an angry mule kicking him. The desert's hot breath swept away the black powder smoke, and through his stinging eyes he saw the first horse was going on—riderless.

The bullet had stopped the buck.

Slocum rose and looked for the woman, but her horse had veered out of sight. Better go see what he could do for her. As he headed down the bank on his boot heels, he wondered again who she might be. With the Remington back in the scabbard, he untied the reins and bounded into the saddle. If there wasn't a nest of the red devils close, he should be able to get her to one of the military forts or stage stops, or even to Tucson, in a day or so.

Out of the draw, he short-loped the roan horse through the waist-high greasewood and brown bunchgrass. Standing in the stirrups, he swiveled around looking for any telltale sign of Indians. Nothing appeared as he scattered some Gambel's quail in his wake. At last, he spotted the woman sitting slumped in the saddle off to his left across a sandy dry wash.

Still cautious, he searched around before he rode on toward her. He could see her dirty, tear-streaked face and the shock written there at the sight of him. She was younger than he had thought—early twenties maybe.

He dismounted and drew his knife. "Howdy, ma'am."

Her blue eyes opened wide at the sight of his approach. She screamed in fear.

He managed to catch the reins of her sweaty, hard-breathing horse, and contained it before it panicked at her outburst. "I'm not here to hurt you. My name's Slocum."

With the knife blade, he slashed the ties that bound her hands to the horn. Then he sheathed the knife and turned his attention to calming her spooked, head-slinging horse. At last, the horse settled down enough that he could turn his attention to the woman. With one arm wrapped around her waist, he swept her skinny form kicking and squalling off the saddle.

"Put me down! Put me down!"

"All right," he said, releasing her on her feet. "Now relieve yourself and get ahold of yourself. We aren't out of this mess yet."

She swept the loose strands of blond curls back with some effort. "How dare you speak to me about such an unmentionable thing."

My lord, this flat-chested, feisty little snob was going to be a handful to save. He caught her by the bare arm and jerked her close to his face. "Listen, lady, I can leave you right here for some red buck to rape you and it'd not bother me one bit. Now do what I say. There is no time for privacy and nice things if you want to stay alive." He released her and started to turn his back.

"Who—who—are—you anyway?" She gathered her skirts to squat.

He led her horse over to his own, allowing her a few feet of privacy. Without turning, he checked her horse's girth. "My name's Slocum. What's yours?"

"Silver—Silver Temple."

"What in the hell are you doing out here anyway?" He slapped the stirrup in place—the cinch was fine.

She pushed down her skirt and used her left hand to

keep the hair back from her eye. "My fiancé, Hyrum Cannon, and I were looking at ranch land."

"Huh?" He narrowed his eyes and peered at her hard, searching for the sanity in that statement. Buying ranch land on some of the bloodiest ground in Arizona?

"A Mr. Bacon was showing us some land that he had listed."

"What happened to those two? Him and your man?"

She blinked, than turned pale as snow. At once, he could see her knees were going to buckle. In two steps, he swept her up in his arms and looked around for a place to put her down. Fainting women—he didn't have time for this tomfoolery.

With the side of his boot, he kicked away the sticks and larger rocks on the ground. Then he laid her down on as smooth place as he could find and held her head in his lap. "Let's start all over."

Her eyes fluttered at him. "They—killed—both of them. It was—horrible." Her bare shoulders shook as she held her hands to her face and began sobbing.

With his free hand, he wrung loose the kerchief from around his neck. "Here, use this."

"Oh, I just want to die . . ."

"No. Get your wits about you and steel up. But we've got to get on the move. This place will soon be crowded with more bucks. Ain't a time to die, it's a time to fight."

"But I don't care—"

He shook her. "Yes, you do. I ain't letting you die or fall into their hands. Now get hold of yourself, girl. We've got to move on."

"But—but—"

He pushed her to her feet and stood. After a quick check around, he discovered she had not made a move to obey him. His impatience with her made him shove her toward her horse. His action caused her head to jerk on her shoulders and she wobbled a few more steps. Then she recovered and staggered over to grasp the saddle horn.

He was tired of her weakness. In three steps, he caught

her under the leg and unceremoniously tossed her on the horse.

"Why you mannerless—" Her red face showed she was affronted by what he'd done.

He ignored her, vaulted on the roan, and reined around to leave. "I told you. No time for niceties. This ain't Saint Louis or New York."

"Why—why, you're—you're indecent."

"No, I'm the guy who's going to save your ass from the Apache. Now follow me." He set his roan northward with the hulking Chiricahuas towering on his right.

His shot had no doubt signaled to a dozen or more of that dead buck's bunch that there was something happening. Slocum pointed north, moved in, and lashed her horse on the butt. At her horse's first jump, she about came out of the saddle, but she grasped the horn tight and pulled herself back as her mount found some hidden vigor. Perhaps the sorrel horse knew that Apaches ate white men's fat horses. The two riders soon were burning the breeze down the wide valley between the Chiricahuas and the Dragoon Mountains.

Slocum wanted to make the stage stop at Dragoon Springs by dark. When his skin started crawling on the back of his neck, he twisted in the saddle to look back. The sight of four riders coming after them only made his stomach curdle into a large rock.

"How many are there?" she shouted.

"Enough," he said, and pushed his mount in close enough to lash her horse again. He knew four of the Apaches were coming hell-bent for an election after them. That skinny girl and Slocum were in for the race of their lives and it all depended on two horses, his stout roan and the sorrel horse she rode, being able to outdistance those mesquite-bean-eating mustangs.

Stakes were down. And they had the lead, but the clubhouse turn was miles away up at the other end of the Sulfur Springs Valley. She began cross-whipping her pony with the reins to make him go faster.

"That a girl," he shouted above the drum of hooves.

Filled with a gut-wrenching dread, he glanced back again. The Apaches were out of sight, but they hadn't given up yet. Traces of their dust boiled into the azure sky. The race had only begun.

"There's a lake ahead." She pointed out the moon lake.

"Playas," he shouted over the drum of hooves. "They ain't deep enough to drown a shy poke."

The look of disbelief she gave him about made him laugh as they raced on northward. That real estate man must have told her there were big lakes nearby. Wouldn't be the first greenhorns who were sold a lakefront ranch. The far-off *kiyi-yacking* over his shoulder told him that, lake or no, they still had Apaches on their heels.

"That rise," he shouted, and pointed to the high point in the west. Perhaps he could stop the Apaches. The horses she and Slocum were riding would soon give out at this pace if he didn't cut them some slack.

She agreed to his directions and swept her sorrel westward. They slid their hard-breathing ponies to a quick stop. He bounded off the roan, tossed her his reins, and jerked the Remington out along with a shooting stick this time. Trigger back, he opened the breech and reached in the saddlebags for a cartridge, talking softly to the still anxious gelding moving around as she tried to hold him.

The cartridge in place, he set up the stick. "Hold your ears."

Rifle balanced on the forked stick, he sighted on the four Apaches charging toward them, and decided at that distance to take out a horse. In the blur of the lens, a black and white piebald came into focus and he squeezed the trigger. The rifle stock jammed hard into his tender shoulder. Wind swept the acrid black powder smoke away and the piebald went facedown, then end over end.

The other riders split to the right and left, and were gone from his sight into the willow growth.

"You—you shot the horse. But why?" She looked shocked and devastated at his actions.

"Tough times call for desperate methods, lady." He

jammed the stick in the scabbard, then the rifle. "I didn't have time to pick my shots. That's it. Now let's ride."

"But, but—" Her lower lip sagged as she handed him the reins.

"We're going north," he said, ignoring her discomfort, and bounded into the saddle. "Better that horse dies than you and me."

"But will that stop them?"

"I doubt it, but it sure gave us a break to wind these ponies. Let's get the hell out of here!"

"But—but you shot it." Thunderstruck, she simply sat her horse like she expected him to beg forgiveness for his act.

"I'll shoot more of 'em, too, if I get a chance. Now ride." He rode in and strapped her horse on the butt.

They short-loped their mounts. Slocum kept an eye on their back trail. Directing her northeast toward the Lordsburg–Tucson stage road, he let the horses drop into a trot. It was a gait they could hold for hours, and would need to. Dragoon Springs was farther away than the station in Apache Pass, but he felt that that station might be ringed by Apaches. Their best chance for some safety, Slocum decided, was Corbett's stop west on the Arizona Stage Line run. Ben Corbett had a rep for handing out either lead or candy that the Apaches took seriously.

When they reached the foot of Texas Canyon, he signaled her to halt, then tossed her his reins to hold. "Stay in the saddle. I want to look at our back trail."

In the growing shadows from the mountain behind him, it was hard to see in the lens any wisp of dust from the Apaches' ponies coming up the stage road after them. From his vantage place on top of the house-sized boulder, he squinted hard. Then a thin fan of dust rose over some live oaks far below them, and he swore to himself while scrambling off the backside of the rock.

"They're still coming?" Her wide blue eyes questioned him as she held the reins.

"They are," he insisted. "If we can make the Springs by

dark, maybe we can fool them." He grasped his saddle horn in one hand and vaulted on his horse.

"Fool them?"

"The Apaches. They hate to fight at night."

She nodded woodenly, turning her horse around. They fled up the dusty ruts of the stage road. A bloody sunset washed the jumbled *malpais* formation that resembled huge toy blocks stacked on each other.

Silver Temple was her name. He glanced over at her dirt-streaked face as she urged on the tired sorrel horse. He saw lots of grit beneath her disheveled hair. He swallowed hard crossing over the pass into the vast San Pedro Valley as twilight softened the harshness of the high desert. With a little luck, in an hour or so he'd be cutting the trail dust out of his throat with some of Corbett's good whiskey.

He glanced over at her. *Silver Temple, whoever you are—we'll be beyond them red devils in a short while.* He urged the roan on.

2

"Slocum, that you, you ole coyote?" The barrel-chested man standing in the doorway's illumination said the word *coyote* like a Mexican. It came out of his full beard sounding *coy-oat-tay*.

"It's me all right," Slocum said, and went around to help Silver down. "We've been dodging some bucks since midday back down in the Sulfur Springs Valley."

"Who's she?"

Slocum heard her suck in her breath, and reached up to catch her. She'd fainted again. With her thin form in his arms, he boosted her up and nodded at her horse. "Catch him. I'll tell you all about it inside."

"She okay?" Corbett asked, catching the reins and leading the sorrel up to the rack.

"She's sunburned to death. Dehydrated, I'd say. I don't know when she ate last. She lost her man and some real estate guy named Bacon to the broncos, and they were fixing to haul her butt off to Mexico when I came along."

"She got a name?" Corbett stepped in alongside him to look at her. "Manuel, take these horses and put them up."

"Thanks. Her name's Silver Temple." Slocum twisted to take her through the door into the lighted eating hall where the stage patrons dined.

9

"Never heard of her. Put her on the table." Corbett indicated the long wooden table.

"No. No," a buxom Mexican woman said, coming from the kitchen while drying her hands on a towel. "Follow me."

Corbett shrugged in disgust. "Hell, all I do is own this place."

"Bring her to a jacal I have for guests," the woman ordered.

"Yeah," Corbett said to Slocum. "The President Grant Suite."

"You don't know who may come here to stay." Acting haughty, the woman swept up a brass candle lamp and led the way out back over the hard-packed caliche to the jacal.

"Consuela, if Grant ever comes out here, some Johnny Reb will put a bullet in his ass before you can even show him your suite."

At the doorway, ignoring his comment, the straight-backed woman looked with concern at the limp girl in Slocum's arms, and then shouted for someone to bring medical things. The room was nice enough. An iron poster bed, dresser, fancy pitcher and bowl, and even a rocker.

Consuela swept back the bedcover and indicated for Slocum to put her down there. When he did and straightened, she herded both Slocum and Ben toward the door.

"This is woman business."

Corbett looked at Slocum and grinned. "Hell, me and you wanted to see what her hatchet ass looked like in the buff."

Consuela boldly threatened him with her forefinger, and he retreated. Both men, laughing, went outside, where they about collided with a short Mexican woman on a mission with a basket. Skirts in her hand, a third, older woman rushed by them, and closed the door at Consuela's order.

"Come on," Corbett said. "If anyone can save her, they will. Besides, I have some good whiskey up there. What brought you here anyway?"

Slocum looked up at the star-studded sky. "I was cutting across from John Slaughter's hacienda headed for Tucson when I saw some buck had her. I got him, and when I went to get her, some others showed up."

"Broncos—been coming up out of Mexico and visiting at San Carlos. I had word from the soldiers out of Fort Bowie that there were a couple of small bands passing through."

Slocum shook his head. "This Silver Temple and her fiancé were looking at lakefront property with a real estate agent called Bacon."

"Playas?" Corbett asked, about to laugh.

"That's what he showed them till the Apaches killed him and her man."

"My pappy said you can go to hell for lying same as you can for stealing." Corbett found the bottle and two glasses. He motioned to the long table and set the tumblers down on the top. Then he uncorked the whiskey and poured some in each glass. Slocum straddled the bench and sat down.

Glass in hand, Slocum saluted his friend and took a sip. The whiskey cut through six inches of dust in his throat. "Those two must be in hell by now. I didn't have any time to go look for them. We were busting our asses to get the hell out of there."

"An army patrol will find them with the help of buzzards. They've got the whole area covered with patrols."

Slocum paused before taking another drink, and looked into his friend's blue eyes. "I never saw any buzzards."

"Oh, they're out there. So are the buffalo soldiers from Fort Huachuca."

"Good."

"Bet you could use some food." Corbett looked around pained. "All them damn women are out there with her."

"I bet I can rustle up something back in the kitchen."

"Come on. Probably get my ass ate out, but we'll find something."

"Consuela runs things?" Slocum smiled and stood up.

"Runs the whole damn stage stop."

They both laughed, and Slocum downed the rest of his glass.

In the kitchen, he found a portion of a browned beef

roast on the countertop. He used a long sharp knife to slice off some of it. Then, from a kettle, he piled some still warm brown beans on his plate. Corbett added several flour tortillas, and they went back out into the eating hall.

"What was in Mexico?" Corbett asked.

"I guarded some gold shipments from a mine in the Madres."

"Tough business."

His mouth full, Slocum nodded as he chewed and at last swallowed. "You ever heard of Henry St. John?"

"No, who's he?"

"Some Mexican bandit I got cross with down there."

"Hmm, Henry St. John don't sound Mexican to me."

"He is, and a bad bandit, too. Take my word. He's all bandit and a cutthroat as well."

"St. John run you out?"

"No, I told my man I needed some more help to stand off this St. John. He refused and I quit."

"And?"

"On the next pack trip that went out, they killed six guards and took the bullion."

Corbett nodded like he understood, and leaned over with the bottle to pour Slocum some more whiskey in his glass. "He offer you a raise to come back to work for him?"

Slocum shook his head as he was busy cutting up the rich meat. "You know those rich Castilians. They would never let it show that they did something wrong. He sent for some more gunhands."

His blue eyes dancing with amusement, Corbett laughed. "Ah, those snotty rich ones are really that way, *mi amigo*. I am never wrong." He struck himself on his proud chest mimicking them.

Slocum nodded. "Señor Valenta is going to find Henry St. John is a formidable enemy."

"But St. John isn't your problem anymore."

With his glass raised in a toast, Slocum nodded.

"So you left your former employer to his own fixings. Did you leave any sad pretty señorita in Mexico?"

Slocum put down his utensils, reared back, and rubbed his palms on his canvas pants. "Ah, always in Mexico, one finds lovely ladies. That is the hard part of living down there." He could even recall her perfume a week later.

"This skinny gringa you brought in wouldn't make a bump on a log beside a fiery Latin one."

Slocum shook his head to dismiss her as only a short inconvenience in his life. He hoped that the flat-chested girl recovered and could be put on a stage to go to her home or her parents. His obligations to the skinny one were over—he'd saved her from the Apaches.

Then, as he went back to rolling up his meat and beans in a tortilla, he considered Señora Lucia Valenta in Sonora, her brown milky flesh, firm breasts, rock-hard nipples, fiery lips, and the molten volcano between her legs. It made his guts roil to even consider her.

"You can have the jacal beside hers to sleep in tonight."

"I am not routing anyone out of their bed, am I?"

"No, the bed is made. Here's to good women." Corbett raised his glass and clinked it against Slocum's raised one. "May God make many more."

"Yes." Then Slocum downed the whiskey. "Many more."

3

A coyote cut loose as Slocum walked under the stars from the stage station to the dark jacal. Corbett had offered him a lamp, but he scoffed at the notion. He was used to moving under the cover of night. The small adobe room that Corbett had provided for him was only a short way from the stage depot, and the soft light in the Grant Suite shone out the open door and windows.

How was the girl doing?

Crickets chirped when he opened the door to his own jacal and went inside. He could see the bed, and began to toe off his boots. Then he hung his gun belt and vest on a wall peg, and pulled the shirt off over his head. Thoughts of a real bed to sleep on made his tight back ache to be on it. He shed his pants. It would be a wonderful night.

He moved the covers back and sat down on the bed to take off his socks and underwear. It was a nice night since, after sundown, the temperature had cooled considerably. Be great for sleeping. He looked up in time to see the door open, and the short Mexican woman slip inside, holding her finger to her mouth to silence him.

"Shush," she whispered. "Consuela is still next door."

"Who're you?"

"Ah, that will be for you to find out." She pulled the

14

blouse over her head. In the room's dim light, he could see her breasts shake as she wiggled the skirt down off her hips. "You don't want me?"

"I never said that."

"Oh, hombre, you will want me." She came over and hugged him around the waist. Her warm lips kissed the corded muscles below his chest. She was very short, maybe four feet three, but feeling her firm breasts pressed against him, he smiled to himself. Dynamite came in small packages.

Her small hand soon reached in and began to jack his rising dick. "Ah, you are *muy grande, cabrón.*"

His head swirled until he reached down and lifted her up so he could kiss her. She wrapped her arms around his neck and her lips sought his mouth like a hungry vixen. Out of breath, she panted as he held her in his arms.

"We need on the bed, my lover. I am on fire for you."

He stood her atop the bed, and she pulled him down on top of her. She raised her short legs and spread them apart in the half-light that filtered onto the bed. Then, with her powerful small hand that grasped his shaft, she guided it into her wet gates. Once he was inside her, she tightly clasped his arms and he went halfway into her.

She cried out, "Oh, *sí.* Oh, *sí.*"

Then he began to probe her tight pussy. Her moans of pleasure were loud enough that he was worried Consuela next door might hear her. With her legs spread out, his hard erection was raking over her nail-like clit going in and out. The contraction soon began to squeeze him, making it harder and harder each time to reinsert himself to the previous depth. Her hunching to meet him helped as the sweat began to lubricate their bellies. Soon, their pubic bones were rubbing on the coarse pubic hair between them and grinding out their effort. He felt a cramp in his left hip, and knew the time was coming. He drove deep. His cum flew out the end of his swollen dick, and she collapsed, her passion spent.

"Oh, hombre," she said, sounding half drunk and shaking

her head as he raised off her. "You are *mucho hombre*. Oh, I am on fire."

"Fire?"

"Yes, you burn me to a crisp."

"That's okay."

She reached over to him. "My name is Donada."

"Slocum."

"I know your name."

"How did you end up here?"

"When I was seventeen, my mother had me marry a dumb boy. His father had some land and cattle, but Arturo was stupid. On our wedding night, he went off and got drunk with his favorite *puta* and left me to cry in his bed. The next morning, he told me to dress, that he was going after firewood in the mountains and I was to help."

She scooted closer, and Slocum put his hand on her breast to feel it. "He was so hung over that I had to drive and he kept falling asleep. Then, when he woke up, he said I had gotten us lost. He recognized none of this country after I had begged him all morning for directions.

"He got off to pee, and three Apaches came out of the chaparral. They killed him, took his gun and all his money, and one of them came over and smiled. He spoke Spanish and said I was his woman.

"Nothing I could do. I hated Arturo, I hated my mother for making me marry him, but I cried anyway. This one who said I was his woman was called Ateez, and he swept me up and took me with them. I was very afraid they would kill me—I had heard so many bad things about them.

"He separated from the other young men later that day, and they teased him in Apache about me, I know. He took me up in a canyon with a small waterfall. There he told me to undress. I told him I had never been with a man. He frowned and smiled. 'Today you will be with a man who appreciates you,' he said."

She paused to raise up, and kissed Slocum on the mouth. Then she pushed her breast at him to tease her nipple some more. Her small hand was caressing his side.

"He appreciated me. We did it maybe six times that afternoon. Each time it grew wilder and wilder, until I finally fainted."

"So you lived with them?"

"For two years. I lost the child I was carrying while running from the *federales*. Then he was killed in a fight in a small town where we traded. I never knew how. Apaches don't talk about the dead. Oh, I mourned for him."

Slocum nodded and slid down in the bed. Raised up, he asked, "How did you get here?"

Then his lips closed on the hard pointed button that capped her right breast. She tasted sweet, like it had been dipped in honey, and she clutched him to her.

"Oh, a gunrunner named Freddie Fine kidnapped me when I was picking berries, and after two weeks of his beatings and him trying to stuff his half-limp dick in me, we arrived here. Corbett said I could stay here and work. He sent that *bastardo* down the road."

Slocum raised up and looked at her. "Corbett send you to me?"

"I am not a *puta*." She sounded indignant.

Slocum raised up on his knees. "I never said that."

"Well." She stretched her arms over her head while squirming on her back. "He did say you would be a good lover if I wanted one tonight."

On his hands and knees over her, he smiled. "Maybe we should try this again."

"Yes," she said, and pulled him down on top of her. "Corbett—he never lied either."

4

In the predawn, Slocum dressed, left her sleeping, and started for the stage depot, a squat adobe building across the small compound. He went in the back door and could smell coffee. Consuela was busy making flour tortillas, but she looked him over from head to toe.

"I suppose you are the reason Marie and I have no help this morning?" Her put-on frown almost made him laugh.

"Was I supposed to wake her?"

"No, I usually do that, but she wasn't to be found in her bed. Marie, get him some coffee."

"Gracias." He took the steaming mug.

"The stage will be here in two hours. But I have the food about ready. You never asked about the white girl you brought here."

"Sorry. How is she?" He'd been so preoccupied with Donada and her body, he'd nearly forgotten about the skinny one. Squatting at the fireplace by the warmth of the glowing mesquite blaze, he blew on his steaming cup.

"I think she will be fine. She asked about you last night and again this morning."

Still squatting, he twisted around to look at the woman. "That's fine. When she gets up, I'll talk to her. I imagine she wants to get back to her own people as soon as she can."

"I think she ran off with this man who was killed. I think her family has disowned her."

He shook his head. Consuela knew more than he did about the woman. Lots more than he did, that was for sure. A woman would tell another woman such things. "What are her plans?"

Consuela shrugged. "I think you."

Slocum nodded slowly. That would never work. He looked, pained, at the two women. "You mean she doesn't think she can go home?"

"I think—how do you say that? She burned the bridge to go back."

"How is she other than that?" He sipped some of the rich coffee. It would clear out the cobwebs.

"Her arms, shoulders, and face are badly sunburned. She's weak from the heat and no water, but she is gong to be fine."

"She awake?"

"She won't want to see you like she is."

"I better go see her anyway."

Consuela made a face of disapproval. "Don't say I sent you."

"I won't." He let the quiet, older Marie refill his coffee cup; then he headed out of the depot and across the compound. He heard the whit-woo whistle of the Gambrel's quail out in the chaparral as his boot soles crushed the fine grit on top of the caliche surface. At the doorway, he cleared his throat and knocked on the open door. "Silver."

"I am not here," she said, wrapped in a blanket in the rocker. No lamp was on in the small room. She sat in the deep shadows.

"Maybe I can talk to her shadow then?" he said, and came inside the doorway to squat on his boot heels.

"Even her shadow is gone."

He could see her try to conceal more of herself under the blanket. "Consulela says that you will heal."

"She's very kind."

"A good woman. What are your plans? I mean when you heal."

"I don't know at this moment. I have little money. I can't live here forever on Consuela and your friend's charity."

"You have anyone you can go and live with?"

"Perhaps my sister Sylvia and her husband Mike."

"Where does she live?"

"Prescott."

"I can get you a stage ticket to there." He paused before sipping his coffee and shifted his weigh to his other boot.

She didn't answer him.

"I mean the stage runs to Prescott. After you heal?"

"I'll consider your offer. What about their bodies? Hyrum and Bacon, I mean. Will the buzzards eat them?"

"Corbett thinks the army patrols will find them or already have found them."

"What will they do with them?"

"Give them as good a burial as they can under the circumstances."

"Sounds very barbaric to me." The rocker's runners creaked as she tried to wrap herself tighter in the blanket. "Where will you go next?"

"Wherever the wind sends me."

She half-laughed. "You hardly seem like a man who has no roots, no estate, no wife and family."

"I have none of those."

"There must be quite a story about that. War record?"

"Captain, cavalry, Georgia. Discharged. Went home to what the federal government called Reconstruction, found ashes and graves, so I went west."

"My, that was condensed."

"Why can't you go back home?"

"My parents planned for me to marry well. I was sent to Mrs. Curry's Finishing School in St. Louis. I returned home to Sedalia and lived the life of the debutante. But somehow, I was bored."

"Bored?"

"Bored to death." She blew out her breath. "I hated teas,

I hated the fake people, I hated it all. My father said I was far too reckless for an unwed woman when I rode horses, and sold my hunter–jumper Velvet in the middle of the season. Then I met Hyrum Cannon. He was married, handsome, bored with his life, he said. His wife Renay was the fainting kind, if you know what I mean."

"You fainted twice on me yesterday."

"Sorry, I never do that. Anyway, you could call me the other woman. We eloped. He planned to divorce her and marry me. Hyrum has a substantial estate. It will no doubt go to Renay. So our dream to start a new life in Arizona has evaporated. My golden goose is gone and all I have are its soiled feathers all over me."

"Nice thing about the frontier. They aren't near as fussy about your past. Why, I bet in Prescott you could find yourself a new life."

"Sylvia called it Preskit."

He nodded. "They call it that up there."

"I can't really face her or any of my family right now. I do want Hyrum's father to know he—he is dead."

"We can telegraph him,"

"Will the army make a report?"

"If they can identify him. Apaches usually take their clothes and anything valuable."

"Oh—" She shuddered, crouched in a tight ball. "I don't regret what I've done. I mean eloping with him." Then, as if repulsed by the notion, she shook her head, making the peak of the blanket wiggle over the top of it. "I have a small photo."

"That might work if we can find the patrol that buried him."

"I have little money to pay you, but I'd like you to go back and see if they buried him and then have the army say that he was the one they buried."

"You know how dangerous that is?"

"You're the only man I know could take me there. I owe him that—Hyrum, I mean."

He dropped to his butt and hugged his knees. "You

could accept the fact that he's dead and go on about your life. Be lots easier than what you're asking."

"I don't have a life—now. It ended when they murdered Hyrum. But I feel responsible for what happened to him. Without me, he might still be home consoling his fainting wife."

"So you want a death certificate?"

"Exactly. Will the wind carry you there?" She giggled and shook her head inside the cocoon. "I can't believe that notion. Here is a picture of him in this locket."

"It could." He pocketed the locket. "You get your strength back. I'll see what I can do in the meantime."

"Slocum?"

"Yes?"

"You won't ever regret doing this for me. I promise you."

He hoped not. "Heal up. Then we'll see what we can do about your life."

"Thank you."

"Don't thank me. Not yet. We haven't done it. It happened west of the playas?"

"Yes. From the empty ranch house, Bacon pointed out the Chiricahuas and the lakes. There is an adobe house, some buildings, and some pens there. Hyrum—he thought or he said we could build a nice house there."

Slocum noticed in the brightening light that she was chewing on her lip. He nodded. "I may ride over there and look for it."

"Oh, I want to go, too."

He didn't need her tagging along. "You get well and heal. We'll see."

"I'll be fine."

He rose. "I am sure you will. Don't rush it."

"I have a little money—"

"I don't need any."

"Must be nice."

"It is. I better see about some things."

"Slocum. Don't go over there without me—please."

"Get well."

She was complaining after him, but he ignored it and headed for the stage depot. Maybe he'd ride back over there later and look for that place where the Apaches had killed the two men. He sure didn't need a skinny tagalong to help him find it either.

"How is she?" Consuela asked when he came back inside the kitchen.

"Recovering nicely." Then he laughed and held out his cup for Marie to refill it. "Yes, she's recovering nicely."

"Did she tell you?"

He blew on the steam. "Yes, she said she had eloped."

Consuela shook her head. "So what will you do?"

"Help her."

"*Bueno,*" she said softly as if satisfied, and went back to her oven with a large wooden spatula to remove the golden loaves of bread. "Get him some butter, Marie. I bet he can eat a loaf by himself." And both women laughed.

"I think you may have murdered our help last night." Consuela delivered two of the loaves to the table. "Donada's never slept in this long before. Has she, Marie?"

"No, Señora, never this long," Marie answered in Spanish, and brought him the bowl of butter.

Slocum thanked her and broke open one of the loaves, and the steam escaped with a powerful smell of sourdough. "You spoil the stage passengers."

"It is the only place they have real food between here and El Paso," Consuela said, wiping her shiny forehead on her sleeve. "The stage drivers tell me that all the time."

Donada arrived and swept into the kitchen. She looked bleary-eyed, and at the sight of him, she frowned.

"Good morning," he said, and gave her a grin. She ignored him and spoke to her boss in Spanish quietly. He knew she had apologized for her tardiness.

"Marie, our helper is here," Consuela announced, and laughed at her words. When the last loaves were out, she handed a long knife to Donada. "You can slice them."

"Sorry I overslept," Donada mumbled after her.

"We know that now." Consuela laughed, going out into the main room.

"Why did you not wake me?" Donada hissed at Slocum.

"You looked so comfortable sleeping."

She waved off his words and went for coffee.

Slocum ate two slices of hot bread and butter, then took his coffee cup outside to listen to the Gambrel's quail and the Mexican mockingbird. Donada was in such a bad mood, she needed to cool off before he said much more to her. Seated on the front porch, he felt the fresh morning breeze sweep his face as he watched the sunrise come over the Chiricahuas. He knew how the Apache felt being moved out of the land they had so fiercely defended against first the Mexicans and later the Americans.

Their spirits lived in this country, which ran from the grassland high desert to the pine-topped peaks where they'd spent the sweltering summers in coolness. They'd had the best of two worlds. They'd sent the Mexican settlers and ranchers packing in Sonora. Vast ranches sat empty below the border, abandoned by their owners after a century of warfare. But not on this side of the border. Anxious land-hungry gringos had moved in, crowding the Apaches onto smaller and smaller and more desolate reservations. The San Carlos Agency was so hot and dry that even the saguaro didn't grow down there. But the Apaches and their plight were not Slocum's problem—unless he ran into more of them like the day before.

"Company," he said aloud over his shoulder at the approach of three wagons. Strange time of the day for wagons to arrive there.

Consuela came out, drying her hands on a small flour-sack towel, to look them over. Each rig was pulled by two teams of mules. The teams were sweaty and shiny in the low sunlight. A couple of armed outriders approached the stage building.

"They must have traveled all night," she said.

Slocum agreed. One way to beat the Apaches, who hated darkness. "You know them?"

"Weldon Thomas's bunch. Mine equipment."

"He come by often?"

"No, he usually cuts down the Sulfur Springs Valley and goes to Tombstone. That's him with the white mustache coming now."

"Why, hello, Consuela, my darling," he said, reining up a stout black horse and giving Slocum a hawk-eyed once-over. Then, wringing an itch in his ear with a pointed finger, he swung down. "We ain't met, have we, mister?"

Slocum stood and nodded at the big man. "Slocum. I'm just passing through."

Thomas hitched up his pants and straightened his suspenders before he nodded back. "Hell, man, that's all any of us are doing in this world. Passing through. Hoping to make another day." Then, observing how his men had stopped the wagons in the center of things, he shouted, "Stupid, get them over to the side. There's probably a stage coming."

"Good," Consuela said, looking at the situation.

"Hell, darling, I wouldn't let them block your stage line business." By this time, he was bear-hugging and trying to kiss her.

Amused, Slocum glanced away. Consuela could handle him. Besides, she probably enjoyed the attention. The two went inside the big room with Thomas's arm familiarly wrapped around her shoulder as he told her how many men he had in his outfit and asked if she could feed them.

"I know," Thomas went on. "I know I should have sent word ahead. But driving at night to get here is serious business and I couldn't spare a man."

Thomas's outriders came in next. Several wore buckskin shirts and pants. They dismounted, pulled down the crotch of their pants, and shoved their .50-caliber Spencers in their scabbards. Slocum knew two of them from his scouting days. Frank O'Day, a braggart from Tennessee whom he'd wearied of quickly, and Luther Vanlett, a Dutch–Cherokee.

"Slocum? That you?" O'Day asked, blinking his eyes at his discovery.

Slocum nodded at the man with the unkempt reddish blond beard.

"Boys," O'Day declared. "Here's one of the greatest scouts I ever worked with. No lie. No lie. Slocum is more Injun than an Injun."

His words drew skeptical laughter from the others, who acted too tired to really care as they plodded through the doorway.

"How've you been?" O'Day asked in his usual anxious manner.

"Fine. Must be valuable stuff in them wagons to have all of you riding shotgun."

O'Day glanced back. Part of his mustache was in his mouth when he started to speak. "Mining stuff. They can afford it."

"Who the hell would steal it?" Slocum asked.

"Damned if I'd know. They just want to be sure it gets there."

"I guess that's so."

O'Day nodded toward the doorway. "I better get in there before they eat all the damned food. Good to see you."

"Sure."

Thomas came out with a cup of coffee in his hand and spoke to his teamsters dragging themselves across the yard. "Better get in and eat. She's got real customers coming."

He turned his attention to Slocum. "Need work?"

Slocum shook his head. "Not today."

"I can use a man with his wits about him."

Slocum shook his head and finished his own cup. He slung the grounds away and went back inside. The crew was busy eating and the two women were handing out platters of fried side meat, bowls of frijoles, and fresh bread.

"Good thing you baked a lot," Slocum said to Consuela as he passed through the kitchen.

"Hmm," she snorted in disgust at him. "That was a two-day supply and they will eat most of it. Don't keep my helper up all night. I'll need her in the morning to bake more."

"I'll keep that in mind." He stopped. She blocked the back door and looked at him with her large round eyes. "Maybe sometime you will need a real woman?"

"Maybe I will—one day." He gave her a promising wink and a smile as the price for his exit. She let him pass.

He saddled his horse and checked the Remington in his scabbard. He'd clean it when he got back. Two shots wouldn't foul it too bad, but it needed cleaning. Must be slipping. He usually did that every time after he fired it. He must have been too tired from his trip out of Mexico and saving Silver's skinny butt. He'd do better, he promised himself. Thinking about Consuela's offer of sex made him smile slightly. He better get going.

He rode out as a stage arrived in a cloud of dust. The Mexican boys who worked for Corbett had the two fresh teams ready to switch. His old friend must have had a bad hangover not to show up for all the action.

Slocum short-loped the strawberry roan, a tough bulldog mountain horse he called Red, for the Texas Canyon. Red stood solid around guns going off and could be ground-tied, and Slocum could guide him with his knees. He was one of those broad-chested horses that could cat-hop up a mountain. In addition, he could run for miles. Tough as rawhide, he was as easy to ride as any horse that Slocum had ever owned, one of those horses that never missed a chance to graze, which made him an easy keeper in the desert.

At mid-morning, Slocum was overlooking the Sulfur Springs Valley. He kept the Dragoons to his right, thinking the place that Silver had talked about was located in this area. A sound made Slocum turn his ear to listen—was it a big flock of ravens? He pushed Red to a rise, and could see the dust and hear the shots. Someone was having a hot fire-fight with some Apaches.

Getting his bearings with the playas and the Chiricahuas, he decided the fight was happening at that ranch she'd spoken about. He could see the outline of the adobe buildings and gray pole corrals when the wind swept some of the blue gun smoke and dust away. It must be the buffalo soldiers from Fort Huachuca.

They looked like they could use some help. He drew his Colt and checked the cylinders. Five shots. He holstered it and reached in his saddlebags for the smaller .30-caliber revolver. It was loaded, too. Satisfied, he stuck it in his waistband. He caught up his reins. *Time to go, old pony. If those blacks don't shoot us for being one of them bronco Apaches, we may get in there to help them.*

He raced Red across the flats, and by keeping to the dry wash, he hoped to slip past the brown shooters and then make a fast burst for the ranch buildings. His plan was working well. Red was churning up the dry sand, when a buck armed with a Winchester repeater ran out and knelt to take aim. It was in that instant the Apache took to get into position that Slocum sighted on him in the rocking gait of the roan and rapid-fired three shots. The Apache was hit in the shoulder, his long gun went off into the air, and he sprawled over on his side.

Slocum kicked Red to go faster past the downed buck and out the head of the draw, knowing that in seconds the mounted braves would be hot on his tail. The soldiers shooting at him were his next problem. "Hold your fire! Hold your fire!"

Several black faces appeared to look hard at him. Seconds went by—no shots rang out, and he rushed into their headquarters satisfied that the shocked buffalo soldiers would be glad to see him.

"You boys getting in some target practice this morning?" Slocum asked the three who ran over to meet him. He dismounted and gave the reins to the first soldier who got to him.

The big sergeant joined them, nodded, and showed his white teeth. "They sure been shooting at us since dawn. We been here all night, and were fixing to head back to our assignment."

"Time we sent them packing." Slocum drew his rifle out and reached in the saddlebag for a cartridge. He pulled out the shooting stick and handed it to the noncom. With the rifle bent over his leg, he cocked the hammer back and opened the rolling block to insert the ammo. When the block was closed, he released the trigger, then recocked. He set the fore stock in the stick and looked through the scope at the hillside covered in century plants.

A buck wearing a red loincloth and rifle stood with his arms crossed up there. Slocum could see the anger and defiance written on his face.

"You's got one in mind?" the sergeant asked, looking at the hillside through glasses.

"One in the red. See him?"

"Yes, sir. I's sure do."

When Slocum's eye was steady on the crosshairs, he squeezed off the trigger.

The rifle's roar made the troopers hold their ears and then cheer. "He's ain't dere no moe."

"Good. Get me another cartridge," he said over his shoulder, and extracted the empty. Blue smoke came out of the bore.

"How far can that gun shoot?" the noncom asked, impressed.

"Clear into tomorrow," Slocum said with the rifle laid over his leg as he reloaded it.

"See that one on the hill?" a private said, looking through the one pair of field glasses they possessed. "One wearing that buffalo hat and sitting on that horse."

Slocum put his eye to the scope and saw the Apache he meant. He cocked the hammer back, steadied the stick. That must be an important one. The report of the shot rolled over the land and "Buffalo Hat" disappeared. His horse raced off, bucking and kicking under an empty saddle.

The shout went up. "They're leaving. They're leaving."

"Where you's come from?" the private asked.

"Dragoon Springs."

A big smile spread over the three dusty dark faces around him. "Well, we sure proud you came to see us this morning."

"Better keep your guard up. They may only be reorganizing," Slocum said to their leader.

"All you men get back on your posts." He turned back to Slocum. "This be your place?"

Slocum shook his head. "No, but did you find two bodies?"

"Yes, sir, we did. A scout from Fort Bowie found them, and they done sent us over here yesterday to bury them."

"Could you tell me if one of them looked like this man?" Slocum took out the locket and opened the cover for him to see the photograph.

"Yes, that sure enough be one of 'em." He handed the locket back to Slocum.

"I need a death certificate for his . . . wife."

"I could send a man with you to swear to it to Fort Bowie and they could make you one, I guess." The noncom looked uncomfortable about the matter.

"I understand. That would be fine." The fact that this man could not read was probably the reason he acted so upset about a certificate.

"Good." His black face smiled back in relief. "My name be Mahaffey and I sure am proud you came here this morning."

"Sergeant Mahaffey, you and your men would have whipped them in time."

"You just speeded that up a whole lot. I better see about my wounded man."

"Yes." Slocum put his rifle and stick back in the scabbard. Then he took the reins from the soldier, a short boy who hardly looked old enough to be in the blue uniform.

"What's your name?"

"Coffee, sir."

"How long've you been in the army, soldier?"

"Six months, sir."

"How many firefights you been in so far?"

"Makes my fourth one."

"Where's your home?"

"Here, sir."

Slocum nodded his head. "I understand. Thank you for holding Red."

"Yes, sir." The short soldier saluted him and ran after his sergeant.

"He may be small, but Coffee he sure be plenty tough," one of the privates said before lighting his corncob pipe.

A bob of dust-floured forage caps from the others backed the soldier's words.

"That sure be a mighty fine hoss you done got dere," the pipe smoker said, appraising him.

"Glad you didn't shoot him," Slocum said, loosening the girth. He slapped down the stirrup. "I held my breath riding in about it."

"Aw, we's ain't got that much ammunition."

They laughed. Then Mahaffey returned and sent them out to scout for any guns, ammo, or loot they could get off the field.

"Sounds like you aren't overrun with ammo either," Slocum said.

"We had ten rounds apiece at the start. We'd done used five and I was planning to let them get well in range to use the rest."

"Ten rounds?"

Mahaffey shrugged his broad soldiers. "We's on spring duty. You know, guarding some small spring over dere at the mountains so dem broncos going back and forth can't get 'em no drink. Army don't think we needs any more rounds."

"They sent you out to bury them, huh?"

"Hey, we's don't mind that. Gets pretty boring sitting up there eating beans and having farting contests."

Slocum chuckled. Mahaffey would do. He and his dozen soldiers were real fighting men. "How is the wounded man?"

"He be fine. He was only creased. Take a lot more'n than that to kill a buff soldier."

"Glad he's okay. Maybe we can catch a loose Injun pony for your man to ride to Bowie with me."

"Coffee. Go tell them we needs a hoss."

"I'm be going, Sarge." The short one took off, his bare feet churning dust for the hillside where the men were checking for anything.

"We got some coffee made," Mahaffey offered.

"Good, I'll take some." With a last look at their reconnaissance, he fell in with the noncom headed for the small fire and the black man squatted beside it.

"Coffee for the man," Mahaffey ordered.

The corporal smiled up at Slocum. "My, my. You sure did make a fine sight dis morning coming out of that draw on dat red hoss. You pistol smoking and that big hat—I said here comes de man going to help us." He laughed and handed Slocum the cup.

"Corporal Johnson here," Mahaffey said. "He was going whoopee when you rode in."

"Thanks and thanks for the coffee." Slocum blew on it. Maybe he'd get this death certificate done for Silver.

"Where you going next?" he asked Mahaffey.

"Oh, back to our spring at the dee base of dem mountains." He indicated the Chiricahuas across the wide valley.

"I'll deliver your man back to the spring tomorrow."

"We's be a back dere then."

"Who's going with me?"

"I's guess Coffee, if'n it be okay?"

"He'll be fine. Who should I report this incident to?"

"Cap'n Green. He be in charge of us now we's so far away from our fort."

Slocum agreed and sipped the bitter coffee. Mostly roasted barley, but he tried to hold his tongue. These men put up with it every day, so he could for one cup.

The trooper found three loose horses. The Apaches took their dead if there were any. One of the ponies had a small bullet wound, but they'd use him for a pack animal and another to carry the wounded man. Coffee was awarded the third, a black paint, and he was promptly tossed into the saddle, ready to go to Bowie with Slocum.

A little past noon by the sun, the two reached the desert mining town of Dos Cabezas. Slocum bought them some meat and bean burritos from a vendor. He left Coffee to eat his lunch and watch the horses while he went inside O'Banyon's Store and Saloon. The dust-floured interior reeked of sour booze and cigar smoke. A grizzly man in an apron met him at the counter side of the business.

"I want two pounds of Arbuckle coffee."

Rubbing his untrimmed mustache with his index finger, the man nodded and went to the shelf for two packages. "You know, I got cheaper coffee."

Slocum nodded, and looked around at the scarred empty tables and the trophy deer and elk horns nailed on the wall over the bar. The whole place was saturated in the gray-blue dust of the mining operations that mushroomed on the hillsides above the cluster of jacales and small adobe businesses.

"Be two dollars."

Slocum paid the man, took his purchases, and headed for the open door.

"That nigger midget out there your servant?"

With a shake of his head, Slocum kept walking. Then he stopped, infuriated at the man's ungrateful comment, and turned to look at the man. "That young man is a soldier who every day risks his life to save your sorry ass."

The man laughed. "I'll sleep better knowing that."

"No, you won't. But some night when a bronco Apache slips up on you sleeping in your bed, in that instant before he slices your throat open, you can always think—where is that buffalo soldier?"

Slocum walked on out, put the coffee in his saddlebags, and nodded to his companion. "Let's head for Bowie."

A hundred yards later, Coffee began to chuckle. "That man back there don't know, but he sure know now."

"How is that?"

"You done told him all about us buffalo soldiers."

Slocum hunched his stiff shoulders and shook his head. "Those folks don't listen."

"They'd been at that ranch dis morning they'd listened."

"Hell, they'd've cussed out General Crook for letting it happen."

In a long trot, they both laughed. Fort Bowie was a few hours ahead. Slocum would be glad to have this matter over with and be on his way. The Apache War wasn't his to worry about anymore. As he looked over the dry bunchgrass and greasewood, he didn't miss it either. He wondered how Miss Skinny was getting along back at Dragoon Springs. Maybe he'd have her paper and be headed back soon.

5

Slocum waited in the main office for Captain Luther Green. A private had retrieved the officer from his quarters. Bowie headquarters was in a log building, the only one in sight. The officer quarters were wood-frame-and-sided houses that looked like they came from a Midwestern town. The long barracks, the stockade, and the stables were Spanish adobe-style. Apache Peak rose above the fort to the south.

When Green, a man in his forties, arrived on the porch, Coffee stood at attention and saluted him.

"What's this about?" Green demanded of the lieutenant behind the desk.

"Sir, Mr. Slocum wants a death certificate for one of the white men that the buffalo soldiers buried today."

"How in the hell can I do that?"

"Private Coffee is here to testify that one of the men they buried is the same as the one in the picture that Mr. Slocum has."

"What's that man doing away from his post?"

"He came to testify."

"I don't give a gawdamn about any death certificate—"

"Captain, my name is Slocum."

With a red-faced scowl, Green glared at Slocum. "I don't care who the fuck you are, mister."

"Maybe General Crook will."

"You threatening me?"

"I don't have to threaten anyone. But at the court-martial, I'll damn sure testify you reeked of cheap whiskey."

Green breathed heavily as if considering his options. "What do you need?"

"Your signature on that sheet."

He scowled at Slocum and then he bent over, took the pen, dipped it in the inkwell, and scrawled his name on it. "That do?"

"No. I want you to requisition some ammo for Sergeant Mahaffey's Company C. They used theirs fighting Apaches at the burial site this morning."

"What in the hell was that all about?" Green asked.

"Major Norman ordered them over there late yesterday to bury two dead white men," the lieutenant said.

"Lieutenant, Company C has a spring to guard."

"Sir, I explained that to the major."

Green turned back to Slocum with a scowl on his face. "Well, citizen, you have your death certificate."

"The ammo?"

"You don't understand about the army—"

"Bullshit. I spent three years with Crook on the Verde. You have a packer tonight take them enough ammo so they can defend themselves."

"You heard the man, Lieutenant, handle it."

"Yes, sir."

Whatever Green mumbled going out the door, Slocum only caught part of it. The silence in the office was loud. Some crickets creaked. The lieutenant cleared his throat. "Reason he didn't know they were sent over there, he was indisposed yesterday evening when the scout came in, and the major handled it."

"Send them eighty rounds per man."

"Eighty?"

"Yes, they fight better with bullets than sticks. Who sends them their rations?"

"Quartermaster, Sergeant Hicks, sir."

"How do I speak to him?"

"Regarding?"

"Rations for Company C."

"Exactly what rations?"

"The beans."

"The army runs on beans, sir."

"Every meal here at Bowie is beans?" He looked hard at the fresh shavetail.

"No, sir."

"That's all they've had to eat."

"What should be done?"

"They need some better rations sent down there. Am I clear?" Slocum reared back and folded his arms over his vest.

"That can be handled, I am certain."

"I do know the general and well. The army has been charged for full rations for Company C and, I imagine, others. Someone is making lots of money off this."

"I'm only a—"

"Lieutenant, I know all about the army."

"Yes, sir. You know these buffalo soldiers don't—"

"Get the attention they deserve. They're fighting men and deserve much more than that. I'm taking Coffee back to his outfit. Thanks for the death certificate."

"At night?"

"Yes, it might be the safest time to go."

"Well, that's right."

Slocum strode out on the porch. "Ready, soldier?"

"I sure be, Mr. Slocum."

At their horses, Coffee leaped on his pony. "You sure done told them about our food."

Slocum laughed and reined his horse around. "No telling, you may get some beef every so often now."

"You reckon so?"

"No guarantee."

Coffee laughed out loud. "No, siree, but it sure made me feel good someone told 'em."

Four hours later under the stars, they were coming up the canyon to the spring.

"Halt. Who goes there?"

"Private Coffee and Mr. Slocum, Roscoe, you dummy."

"Sarge he say I supposed to challenge anyone comes up here."

"Can't you tell us from Apaches?"

"It's dark, Coffee. You don't understand."

"Never mind. Bet we's can find us some beans. That jerky you gave me was good, but my old belly wants some beans."

Mahaffey was up and met them by the campfire. Coffee brought Slocum a plate of beans. Slocum was busy giving Mahaffey the Arbuckle coffee he'd bought them.

"Wow," the noncom said, sounding impressed. "This almost be better than good whiskey."

"Almost," Slocum said, and took the plate of hot beans. Then he sat cross-legged on the ground eating his midnight meal, and told the sergeant about his experience at Bowie and his complaints about their rations.

"Don't know if it'll do any good, but I tried," said Slocum.

"My, my, ammo and food. Guess we gets all that, we be like kings up here." Then Mahaffey laughed. "By the way, the men think the one with the buffalo hat you shot was their medicine man named Carron or something like that."

"Never heard of him."

"We ain't sure he was killed, but he sure be plenty wounded, huh?"

"Yes, he sure could be," Slocum agreed between spoonfuls of his food. The beans weren't bad when seasoned, but as a steady diet they could get tiresome as hell. "I'm going to get a few hours' sleep and get back to Dragoon. I have the certificate. Thanks."

"You ever want to help us again, you ride right in."

"I hope they bring ammo tomorrow with the food."

"Oh, they will—someday." Mahaffey laughed.

"I told them fighting Apaches with sticks wasn't the answer."

"We sure appreciate you."

"No, I appreciate you and your men. This isn't great duty. But denying them the springs makes it that much harder for the broncos to go back and recruit more young bucks."

"That be our job."

"Thanks for the food. I'll get a few hours' shut-eye."

After a day of lounging in their camp, a little past sundown he was short-loping westward across the Sulfur Springs Valley, the moon slowly coming from behind the vast Chiricuhua range.

He wondered about Donada. Maybe she got up in time today to help Consuela bake her bread. At least he had Silver's certificate for Hyrum's father. Something was unsettling about hearing a loved one is dead and not ever getting proof. Bereaved people can think all kinds of things, like maybe their loved ones were not really dead.

He arrived at Dragoon Springs before daylight. The morning star over his left shoulder told him dawn was over an hour away. Dry-eyed and numb, he unlaced the girth, swept off the saddle and blankets, then put Red in the corral with some of the stage line horses. He slung his saddle on a rack in the tack room, leaving the saddle blankets unfolded on top to dry. He stopped at the water trough, took off his hat, and used handfuls of water to rinse his sore face. Then, with his kerchief, he dried off. The morning coolness found him and swept his cheeks as he started for the main building.

He paused in the doorway and noted that one lone candle lit the kitchen. No one was in sight when he stepped inside.

"Ah, you have returned," Consuela said, carrying a sack of flour into the room from the pantry. Setting it on the table, she swept the white powder off her sleeves with her hands.

"Can I help you?" he asked.

She nodded and motioned at him to follow her. She went down the steep stairs and he followed. The cellar reeked of onions and peppers. Some slabs of salt pork wrapped in cheesecloth hung on hooks.

He almost collided with her. She blew out the candle on the shelf, then slipped her arms around him. She pressed her large breasts into him, the swell of her belly keeping him from pressing his privates at her.

Her fingers fumbled with his gun belt and she set it on the ground. She moved back against him, her open mouth covered his, and her hot tongue began to lash his mouth until their lips separated so they could catch their breath.

"You have been away for too long, my darling," she said. "Our time is short, others will be coming soon." Her palm rubbed over the mound under his pants between them. With a wink at her discovery, she dropped to her knees before him, unbuckling and tearing open his fly.

When she took the shaft of his dick in her firm fist and inserted the head in her mouth, he stood on his boot toes in response. Her alternate sucking and licking soon had him breathing so rapidly, he could hardly restrain himself. With his cock in and out of her lips, and her rubbing the skintight head on the hard surface of the roof of her mouth, his hips were urging him to shove it down her throat. Her left hand began to massage his scrotum. He knew he couldn't contain it any longer, and his gun went off. She dropped back on her heels and wiped her mouth on the back of her hand.

"Same ole Slocum," she said, and he lifted her up. Then he buttoned his pants.

At the sound of someone moving around upstairs in the kitchen, she quickly took down a slab of bacon and whispered, "Take this up for me."

"Yes, ma'am, anything else?"

"Give me a match. This damn light's went out."

He struck one and relit the candle. Then he packed the bacon upstairs.

"Morning, Marie," he said, exiting the cellar.

The older woman nodded, barely looked at him as if she was minding her own business, and made herself busy adding coffee to the boiling water. He put the slab of bacon on the wooden preparation table.

Soon, Consuela came up the stairs still huffing. "That cellar is a lot of work going and coming up and down."

Marie agreed, and put the lid back on the coffeepot. "I think there are spirits down there, too." She crossed herself.

"Oh, what kind?" Consuela began to pile flour on the table with a large cup.

"I am not sure," the old woman said. "Trust me, I know about spirits. I can feel them down there."

"You feel any spirits down there?" Consuela asked Slocum.

"Oh, yes," he said, straddling a chair backward and overseeing her work. "I could feel them."

Donada came in and smiled at discovering that he was back.

"When did you return?" she asked, putting the shawl she came in with on the peg.

"Ten minutes ago."

"Any more Indian trouble?"

He shook his head. "No problem this time. Some buffalo soldiers had a problem with a small band over in Sulfur Springs Valley."

"Oh, that is close."

"The Indians ran away again."

"But where?"

"Damned if I know. They left was the good thing."

"You tell him about the message?" Donada asked Consuela.

The woman shook her head. "They sent word yesterday that bandits killed the man you use to work for—Valenta," she told Slocum.

"Anything else?"

"Yes, his widow wants you to come and help her."

"Who brought the message?"

"A boy name Largo. He's sleeping in the barn."

"Yes, I know him."

"What will you do?" Consuela had a large wad of dough she was kneading in her hands.

"I guess go and help her."

"What about the girl you brought here?" Consuela asked. "She tells us she has no one."

"I'll fund her passage to her sister in Prescott."

The three nodded in approval as if relieved at his words.

"Get the man some coffee," Consuela said to Marie. "He's been up all night riding to get back here."

Slocum nodded. So Valenta was dead. Served him right. Slocum had told the man that the bandit St. John was going to get tougher and tougher. Blowing steam off his cup, he wondered about Valenta's wife Lucia. She had sent that boy Largo to find him. That meant she really needed him. He'd better grab some sleep and get on his way back to Mexico.

6

"Wake up. Wake up."

He opened his matted eyes and in his unclear vision could see the girl Silver was on the bed shaking him.

"What is it?"

"Apaches attacked the freight wagons."

"Huh?" He could see the buckskin-clad O'Day standing behind her. "Get the damn army. That's their job." Still not completely awake from his deep sleep, he sat up. "When did it happen?"

"Daybreak," O'Day began. "They swept in. Maybe two dozen of 'em. Who can tell, it was fast. They got Thomas and three of the teamsters in the first surge. Used arrows when they first attacked. I guess that's what surprised us. Plenty silent. Whack, whack. Then when the damage was done, four of our guys down, they came screaming with new Winchesters and wounded more."

"What can I do?"

"That mining equipment is worth a lot of money and they need it at Tombstone. I figured if you were here, I'd see if you'd organize the deal and get it there. I'm sure they'd pay us well for doing it."

"They never burned the wagons?" Slocum asked, looking at the anxious-faced girl sitting on her heels close by.

"No, all they got was the stock."

"You must have fought like hell to save them."

"We did. There's enough teamsters and workers to get the equipment to Tombstone. Can't take us much over four days to move it over there."

"Telegraph wire up?" he asked Silver.

She shook her head. "I don't know."

"It's working," Ben Corbett said, coming in the doorway.

"O'Day, wire Bowie." Slocum started to sweep the covers back, and then he looked at Silver. "I'm getting up."

"I won't look."

"Good," he said, and swept the covers fully back. "Tell Bowie they attacked the wagon train and killed Thomas."

Corbett nodded. "Where are you going to get enough stock to move the equipment?"

"Damned if I know. Going through St. David instead of Benson, I can cut almost a day off. But finding enough draft animals may be the tough part."

"Short of Tucson, I think so."

"I hope to find a freight outfit coming out of down there."

"Corbett?" O'Day stuck his head back in. "Those women say you operate the key."

"I'm coming." He turned back to Slocum, who was standing. "Lots of luck."

"I may need it." He watched Corbett leave. He pulled his britches up and buttoned them, aware that Silver had moved to sit on the edge of the bed and was kicking her legs like she was on a swing.

"I have your death certificate," he said.

She nodded and did not look up. "Sorry I woke you. But Mr. O'Day said it was urgent."

"No. I needed to get up. You all right?"

"As right as I can be."

He dropped beside her on the bed and shook out a boot. No need to put it on with a scorpion or vinegaroon in the toe. "You need to go visit your sister."

"No." She rubbed her palms on top of her legs, which were under the dress they must have found for her. "I'm going along with you."

"You don't understand—"

"I understand perfectly. You saved me. You can keep me." With her lips set in a tight line and her fists clenched in her lap, she sulked.

"You have no idea where in the hell I need to go." Picking up his other boot to shake it out, he looked over at her.

She never returned his gaze. "Benson, I figure, to get teams, right?"

"Then we've got to snake them into Tombstone."

"Two, maybe three days. What then?"

"You'll be on the stage to Prescott."

"No, we're going to Mexico."

He strained on the mule ears to pull the second boot on. "No way. Mexico is too dangerous."

"If the Apaches had gotten me, I'd've been in Mexico."

He shook his head and clapped his knees. "Lunch over?"

"I'm sure they have some food."

"Let's go get something to eat." They could talk about her going to Prescott later.

"You want Red saddled while you do that?" she asked.

"Sure."

"I'll have him and a horse for me saddled while you eat."

Hell, she could go to Tombstone, Slocum decided. Then he'd send her packing. "All right. Where's Largo?"

"Is he going, too?"

"No, I need to send a message to his boss."

"I'll find him. He's probably still sleeping. Said he rode night and day to get up here and find you."

"Thanks."

In the main building, Corbett worked on the telegraph key. O'Day stood above him and nodded.

"He getting out?" Slocum asked.

"I think so."

Corbett nodded to reassure him. "I'm getting a message back."

"Good," Slocum said, heading for the kitchen. "I'm getting some food. Silver's saddling horses."

"Lieutenant Gauge—sends his regards—says that they sent ammo and—food to Company—C." Corbett continued listening to his key. "They will have two companies here in the field by nightfall."

Slocum shook his head. Hell, that bunch of Apaches would be miles from there by then. "It'll be a big help."

Corbett took off his headset. "I agree. But what else can we do?"

"This hit-and-run business by the broncos needs to be matched with teams of Apache scouts in the field. Crook knows it. His boss, General Sherman, disagrees with him."

"Well, Crook has handled them before."

"He can do it like that," O'Day agreed.

"Things keep getting worse," Corbett said. "Instead of better."

"That and the economy. Which has kept the railroad from crawling through here and putting you out of business," Slocum said.

"It'll come, I know," Corbett agreed, and looked hard at the dirt floor.

"Then what'll you do?" O'Day asked.

"Hell," Corbett said, looking up at them. "I was looking for work when I found this deal. You taking over moving the equipment?"

Slocum nodded. "You said they'd pay well to get it. I'll do it."

"They will."

"I'll get some food in my belly, then we can go look for teams." Slocum went into the dining room.

"Ah," Consuela said. "You are hungry again?"

"Always for your cooking."

"Bread. I have some lamb stew." She stood hands on her hips, her brown eyes challenging him.

"Mutton?"

"Lamb."

"I'll take some."

"O'Day?" she called out to the scout. "You eating, too?"

"Yes, ma'am."

"You going to help that bunch?" Consuela motioned to O'Day.

Slocum nodded. "Those mines need that freight. They'll pay the bill."

She started to say something, then ran her lower lip under her even upper teeth. "What about Silver?"

"She's going along," Slocum said, and took off his hat.

"I see how you got her on the stage for Prescott." She laughed at his plight, and went back in the kitchen talking loudly to her crew about all the special meals they had to fix. Then they all laughed loud enough that both men heard them.

Corbett joined them with a bottle of whiskey. He drank, they ate. Slocum had noticed the man's absence from other events earlier. The man was deep into drinking, but Slocum wasn't his keeper. Some folks drank to forget; others drank because they weren't satisfied with their place in life—the rest wanted to escape. Whiskey didn't answer any of them. He'd tried it. It only numbed the rough edges of life.

Silver came in and joined them, refusing food since she had eaten earlier. Her blond hair was gathered in a bun in back. The red remains of her sunburn still scarred her face. They'd heal, but he'd need to get her to wear a wide-brimmed hat.

In the kitchen doorway, Consuela, seeing the boy come in, ordered more lamb stew for him.

"Ah, Largo," Slocum said. "Have a seat. Food is coming."

"*Gracias,*" Largo said to Consuela.

"Tell 'em about the *patrón,*" she said to Largo.

"Those *bandidos* have robbed the last two trains." Largo looked at Slocum to see if he knew that. Then, as Slocum nodded, he continued. "The señora, she told him he should get you to come back." The handsome boy shrugged his shoulders. "He never listened to her. The *patrón* said he would stop the *bandidos* himself. They killed him and took the gold."

"The same bandits?"

"I think so. The señora said for me to find you and get you to come back and work for her."

Slocum nodded. "Tell her I will be coming in ten days. Not to ship any bullion until I get there."

"I savvy," the boy said, and a smile crossed his face. "She will be very happy that you return. So will the men at the mine."

"You be very careful going home. If those bandits learn that you have a message for her, they'll kill you."

"I know. They are mean men."

"Largo, do you have money for your food and horse feed?"

He swallowed. *"Sí, señor."*

Slocum started to dip out a spoon of stew and paused. "Good. Just watch yourself night and day."

"I will."

He went back to eating.

"Damn, Slocum, you're going right back into that mess down there?" Corbett scowled in disapproval at the notion, then raised his glass. "To your health, old buddy—may those fucking *bandidos* not cut out your balls and kill you."

Slocum raised his spoon. "I'll drink to that."

Corbett nodded and then, acting upset, took his bottle and glass. He headed for the door. Slocum watched his longtime friend disappear. Corbett had problems. But Slocum wasn't sure what they were. Might be the railroad coming and putting him out of business—something.

Consuela came into the room, noticed Corbett was gone, and looked at Slocum. "Corbett's son was killed in Mexico a year ago. He has not been himself since then."

"Who killed him?" Slocum asked, buttering a chunk of fresh bread.

She wrinkled her nose. "If he knows who, he never tells us."

"A son?"

"He didn't know of him. The boy came here to meet his father. He told him that his mother on her deathbed said that Corbett was his real father. Corbett could not deny him." Consuela shook her head. "He looked so much like him—"

"The boy stay here?"

"For a while. Then he said he must go back to see his family down there. Corbett gave him money and told him to come back after he saw them. The boy agreed."

"Where did they kill him?'

"They said in a cantina in Santa Madre."

"No name for the killer?"

"No. It eats at Corbett that he did not go down there and avenge his death. I know it does."

Slocum nodded slowly. "Why didn't he?"

"You see him shake?"

"Some."

"Well—" She looked around to be certain Corbett was not around. "He couldn't shoot a gun fast enough because of that."

Under the table, Slocum pushed his palms over the top of his pants legs. He closed his eyes for a moment to push away the notion. One day he'd face the same situation, if some gunman didn't end his life before then. *Damn.*

7

Slocum, Silver, and O'Day reached Benson at dark. After checking on the crew at the wagons, they rode on to their destination. The two wounded teamsters had only sustained minor injuries and all would recover. They acted pleased that Slocum had taken on the leadership since they were counting on making the delivery so they could collect their pay for the six-week job.

Benson was a small, sleepy settlement on the San Pedro River and the emigrant trail. Slocum and O'Day left Silver with the horses and went inside the first cantina. The bartender was a big man with a black mustache.

"Slocum's my name. I'm looking for teamsters. Apaches took our horses and mules this morning," Slocum said.

"Hartley's mine. Heard about it. Said they killed Thomas?"

"Yes. I need six teams of mules to get the freight over to Tombstone."

"That'll be tough. There ain't that many good teams in the country."

"Not any freighters left in the country?"

"No." Hartley shook his head. "Apaches got them all scared out of here. Thomas, he was tough. And he'd always made it up till now. But they got him, too."

50

"Hell's fire," O'Day said. "There's got to be some teams we can hire."

"I guess tomorrow we go up to Tombstone and see if the mine owners can find us some draft stock," Slocum said.

Hartley looked at the smoky ceiling for help. "Good luck, men."

"From the sounds of things, we'll sure as hell need it." O'Day drew up his shoulders and started for the door.

Slocum thanked the man and followed O'Day outside.

"Do any good?" Silver asked, rising in the stirrups and grasping the horn in the darkness.

"None here," Slocum said, and jerked his cinch tight.

"What now?" she asked him.

"We'll ride down to St. David and see how many farmers we can hire."

"Them Mormons are clannish as hell," O'Day said under his breath. "I don't trust 'em."

"Our best choice. Besides, Mormons also like money."

That night, they camped by the sluggish San Pedro, and in the morning, after some jerky for breakfast, they crossed the wooden bridge into St. David. Slocum stopped them at the small store, dismounted, and went inside. A short, attractive, gray-headed woman greeted him at the store and he asked for direction to the bishop's place.

"Oh, you mean Bishop Rutherford."

"Yes, ma'am." He'd had no idea of the man's name until she told him.

"Go down this road to the first big place with honey hives. That's his."

"Thank you."

Slocum and his crew rode down the road, turning in at the beehives. In a white shirt and tie, Rutherford came out on the porch.

"Bishop." Slocum stepped down, pushed his hat back with his thumb. "Slocum's my name. Apaches struck my freighting outfit yesterday. Killed a few of the men and stole our horses and mules. We have three heavy wagons. Been pulling them double teams with some big mules and horses."

"What can I do for you?"

"They're on top of the grade above Benson. If you and your people can get them to Tombstone in thirty-six hours, I'll pay you three hundred dollars in gold."

"What if it takes longer than that?"

"Two-fifty in forty-eight hours."

Rutherford, a tall man, began pacing his porch as if in deep thought. "Cash, mind you."

"Cash."

"Those wagons are all sound?"

"Sound as a ship," O'Day said from his horse.

"Three hundred dollars and we'll deliver in thirty-six hours from the time we leave up there. I may need three teams to a wagon after we get off the grade to pull that much load. Many of our teams are not large horses."

"Your business, you can hook four to them, I don't care. Deliver the wagons."

"We can do that." They shook hands.

"We'll be ready to roll."

"Good. We'll be there at sunup," Rutherford said.

Slocum nodded and went to get on his horse. The last thing he heard was Rutherford telling one of his towheaded boys to go down and ring the bell, that they needed to have a council meeting.

A few hours later, they rode on to Tombstone with O'Day still shaking his head over the deal. "You'd never get a teamster to work for that kind of money knowing you were in a crack."

"What did I tell you?"

"Them Mormons like money."

Slocum winked at Silver.

"You see his daughters?" she asked them.

"Those were his wives, girlie," O'Day said.

"Wives?"

"Yeah. Mormons marry 'em young and lots of them."

"You think so, Slocum?"

He nodded. "O'Day's right. They believe in that polygamy."

Silver shook her head in disapproval.

"You don't like that?" O'Day asked her, waiting for an answer.

"No."

"My, my." O'Day laughed. "Guess we won't get you married off to a Latter-day Saint like we planned."

"Busted up our plan," Slocum said. "Let's trot. We need to see this mine company and get back."

"That's fine," Silver said, booting her horse. "I'll find my own man. Thank you."

"I sure didn't mean to make you mad," O'Day said.

"I need a man, I'll get one. Don't make any plans for me."

They reached Tombstone past noontime, and went to the Silver Rock Mining office. Slocum dismounted and went inside. A young man showed him to the office of the mine manager, Mark Shelton.

Shelton rose from behind his paper-covered desk and shook Slocum's hand. "What can I do for you today?"

"Slocum's my name."

"Mark Shelton's mine. Have a seat." He indicated a chair.

"Your mining supplies are on the mountain above Benson. Apaches attacked it yesterday."

"Oh, hell—" Shelton slapped his forehead.

"Thomas is dead. Three others. They took all the horses and mules."

"The parts I have ordered? The air hammers?"

"They're still in the crates and fine."

Shelton collapsed in his chair. "Thank God."

"I've hired the St. David Mormons to bring the loads in here since the Apaches took all the stock. They'll cost you."

"How much?"

"Three hundred dollars for delivery here in thirty-six hours."

A small chuckle rose in Shelton's throat. "What do I owe you?"

"Two hundred for my part."

"Small price to pay." Shelton rose and went to the great

safe. He spun the combination wheel, and the door came open. "Gold or paper?"

"Three in gold for them. I'll take paper."

"You taking over Thomas's business?" Shelton asked, putting a small canvas sack on the desk. "Double eagles."

"I'm sure that Rutherford will be happy with that."

Then the man stacked the money in paper twenties on his desk. "Well, are you happy enough to take it over?"

Slocum shook his head and looked out the window at the small quaking cottonwood someone had planted. He'd not take root anywhere—couldn't.

With thanks, he took the money and shoved it in his pants pocket. "See you in forty-eight hours or less."

"You think they can make it that fast?" Shelton looked amused.

"Don't get in their way is all I can say. They round those Dragoons, they may be here in twenty-four."

"Whoever hired you sure knew their business. I'd never thought about those Mormons doing that. Wish you'd reconsider my offer."

Slocum lifted the moneybag. "No, thanks. Oh, a man named O'Day will settle up for Thomas's part and to pay the men."

"Thanks." Shelton shot a hand out to shake with Slocum. "I'll look for their dust coming down the valley."

Outside, O'Day stood by their horses. "How did you do?"

"Got the bishop's money." He held up the sack in his left hand. "And he paid me so you won't have to."

"Hell, how did you do all that?"

"You asked me to get this job completed, right?"

"I sure did. And damn, you done great."

"Thomas got any heirs?"

"I don't reckon he ever mentioned any."

"Well, you might inherit all of it."

"Huh?"

"Shelton wants someone to keep hauling to him from the railhead."

"You giving me the wagons?"

"No." He winked at Silver. "I'd say they just fell into your hands."

"Heavens, O'Day, you may even get rich," she said.

"Hell, I'd try anything. Guess I could do it."

"We sit around here palavering all day, we won't meet them at the wagons." Slocum looked around at Tombstone. Most of it was rebuilt since the last town fire. The smell of pine sawdust hung in the air. They left the town in a long trot for the distant wagons.

Slocum was not surprised when they reached the train past midnight and several hipshot teams were hitched around small campfires under the stars.

"They're already here," Silver said, sounding shocked as they rode through them.

"Hell, he told you about them," O'Day said. "This'll be your chance to get a man."

"No, thank you."

Dismounted, Slocum took loose his bedroll and handed Silver a blanket. "Here, you'll need this if you don't have a man to keep you warm."

"Thank you. I'll do that quite adequately. How far did we ride today?"

"Let's see, we started at St. David. Oh, fifty miles or more."

"No wonder I'm so sore." She rubbed her hip.

"You can go back and stay at Dragoon."

"Go back?" She wrinkled her nose at him. "I won't miss it for anything."

"I'm sleeping over there." He pointed to a spot.

Hugging the blanket, she nodded. "I'll be close in case *hell* breaks out."

They both chuckled. O'Day had already gone off to find his own bedding.

Dawn was making the horizon rosy when they hooked their small mustang teams to the wagons. Three teams to a wagon, and a driver rode the wheel horse. Thomas's crew was divided up to ride in the three units, since O'Day had the only the horse they'd recovered. The bishop rode a leggy black beside the first wagon as they rolled out.

Once their brakes were kicked off, the heavy wagons rolled easily downhill and the horses held a good trot coming off the mountain. Slocum knew this was the easy part. It would be the hills in the valley that would pull the guts out of them.

Three hours later, fresh teams replaced the first ones. Some young boys on horseback led the used teams behind the wagons. No doubt the bishop had it in mind to reuse them later. The initial grades slowed the wagons, but the drivers decided not to use more horses, making up some time going downhill.

At noontime, more fresh teams were waiting, standing beside the road, and they were hooked to the wagons. Slocum passed out more jerky to Silver and O'Day, and they washed it down with tepid canteen water. Silver dismounted and ran up an arroyo to relieve herself.

"The drivers must have big bladders," she whispered to Slocum when she returned.

"They did it when they switched teams," Slocum replied.

"Hell," O'Day said, riding over to rejoin them. "They'll be in Tombstone by dark at this rate."

Slocum looked back at the Dragoon Range. They were already near the place where Cochise had signed the peace treaty with General Howard years before. They might set some kind of record if those tough ponies of theirs held up.

"Three o'clock they make the last switch," Silver said. "I heard the boys say so. The bishop sent a boy on a fast horse an hour or so ago to tell them to move that relay closer to town. So we're going faster than he even planned on."

"You bet, girl. They'll be there by dark. Maybe fifteen hours."

"Hell, they ought to give us a discount."

Slocum shook his head. "I'm just glad it'll be over."

She closed her eyes and stretched her back. "I'll damn sure have been in the saddle long enough by the time I get there."

With a nod, Slocum agreed. Far across the valley, he could see through the heat waves to where, on top of a mesa, sat the buildings of Tombstone.

The Mormons changed horses in record time. Silver came running from the dry wash. "What's all the shooting about?"

"Tombstone don't need much to celebrate over."

"My heavens, how did they know the Mormons would deliver it today?"

"Called a Deseret telegraph."

"No one has wires."

"They don't need 'em."

"We getting a room in Tombstone? I could sleep for a week."

"Sure."

"Just get one," she said.

He nodded and booted Red. His once-stout pony could use a rest, too. One room. Lay over for a day, then load her on the stage for Prescott. He had work to do in Mexico. Lots of it.

8

Shelton joined them on the dock, shaking his head in disbelief. Firecrackers were popping off all over town, and like a rooster Mayor Clum took charge of the situation. "Ladies and gentlemen. Forty-eight hours ago, these wagons were being attacked by bronco Apache. Look here, there are still arrows in the sides of these wagons. But they were defended by brave men who managed to save these important loads of parts and much-needed mine machinery.

"Folks—folks, listen. These wagons left the emigrant road up by Dragoon Springs this morning. And by relays, right? They all came down here today, so no shift time was lost waiting for these valuable parts."

More firecrackers. More cheering. Slocum nodded to Silver and they turned their horses through the crowd for the OK Corral Livery. Their tired horses were left there with orders to grain them and give each one a rubdown. Then, with her on his arm, Slocum and Silver hurried to Nellie Cashman's Resturant for a real meal that Slocum had promised her.

"What about O'Day?" she asked, looking back over her shoulder as they maneuvered through the crowded boardwalk.

"We'll let him get all that applause. He'll be busy anyway

58

settling up with the crew. O'Day's all right, but I get enough of him very quickly."

"You gave him the freight business. Surely, you could have settled Thomas's estate and had a good business until the railroad gets here." She glanced over, looking bewildered at Slocum.

He guided her past two drunk miners floured in dust who were, by his appraisal, trying to consider if she was a dove or his wife. He lowered his voice. "I couldn't have hung around and run it."

"Oh?"

"Long story. Later." He opened the door to the restaurant and showed her inside.

"My," she said, looking around the well-appointed eatery. "This is like stepping into something at home."

Slocum nodded and gave the hostess his hat.

"Booth or table?"

He shook his head, patting down his hair with his palm. If you wanted to be less conspicuous, you took a booth for yourself and your mistress. He hardly considered Silver his mistress. In fact, he didn't even consider her half the time. She wasn't whiny, and most of the time she was hardly noticeable. It amazed him how she seemed to enjoy it all. Her butt must no doubt be sore after all the hours they'd spent in the saddle. Slocum looked across the room at a gambler he knew—Johnny Kline. Fort Stockton. Texas. He'd once showed the shocked dandy a royal flush of hearts. Slocum smiled at Silver. "Ready to eat?"

"Famished."

"Roast beef," he said. "They know how to fix it. Slice it thin and it will be wonderful."

"Fine. Are there bath facilities at the hotel?"

"We can order a tub and hot water up to the room."

She looked very seriously at him. "How much will that cost?"

He waved off her concern and spoke to the waiter dressed in a formal suit and tie. "Roast beef and . . ."

Two hours later, the high-back copper tub sat in the

middle of their Palace Hotel room. Buckets of steaming water sat on the floor beside it.

"You want me to leave so you can bathe?" he asked, sitting on the edge of the bed.

"Of course not." She began to unbutton the dress.

"Suit yourself."

"Slocum, there are times you can be delightful and times I think you'd drown me."

He chuckled. "Guess I have Mexico on my mind."

"Oh, yes. The mine owner." She shrugged off the dress and tossed it on a chair. Then she looked at him, shrugged, and untied the petticoat at her waist. "Are you going to pour the water in for me?"

"Yes, ma'am." He rose as she sat on the chair in the buff and unbuttoned her shoes. Her thin body looked snowy-white with her teacup-sized breasts capped by pink nipples as she removed her footgear. He added part of the water to the tub, and she used him for a support to test the temperature with her toe.

"Too hot?" he asked.

"No," she said, and stepped in with her hand on his shoulder. Then she leaned out and pursed her lips for him.

He kissed her. Then she winked mischievously at him and slid down into the water with a moan. "This feels so— so wonderful."

"Good," he said from the open window, and looked down at the busy street masked in dust and the gathering sundown. How was he going to tell her this was the end of the trail for the two of them?

Come morning, she'd have to be on the Benson stage for Prescott and he'd be trailing a packhorse behind Red headed for Mexico. Damn border outlaws anyway. Henry St. John. A rough upstart who planned to live outside the law. Bribe some locals. Shoot a few resistant individuals and take over an entire region. Followers were easy to find. Then they could drink all day in a cantina and squeeze the tits of any *puta* they wanted to instead of following an oxen or donkey with a plow and raising corn in a dry unyielding plot.

She stood up, and water cascaded off her slender form. "Your turn."

"I'll rinse you."

"Thanks." She smiled, hugging her small breasts with her arms.

"Oh," she said as he poured the pail over her.

She took the towel to dry herself and stepped out. Her blue eyes followed his every move as he toed off his boots, shucked his gun belt, and unbuttoned his pants. He pulled his suspenders down and shed his pants while she sat in the chair and dried her feet.

"Never been married?" she asked.

"No." He had his back to her and was unbuttoning his shirt.

"No wife, no roots. Wanted?"

He turned and nodded. "Kansas."

"What for?"

"Shooting someone who asked for it."

She nodded slowly as if she was considering the matter.

He stepped into the tub. The water was still warm. He sat down with his knees practically under his chin. She came over and picked up the brush. "I'll scrub your back."

"Fine."

"And you ride across the West rescuing maidens in distress like a knight from King Arthur's court."

He chuckled at her words. "They're hard to find, too."

"Well, I'm glad you spared me the experience of becoming a squaw." On her knees, she applied the bristled long-handled brush to his back.

"Feels good."

"Good. You are a mystery to me." She leaned forward and kissed him.

"How is that?"

"I understood you quit this man because he would not

give you the help you felt you needed, and now you go back to help his widow."

He threw his shoulders back and flexed his stiff back. "It wasn't her fault her husband was a skinflint."

"I see." She moved in front of him and caught him by the nape of the neck. Then she kissed him hard, and her other hand dove into the tub to find his tool as their lips meshed. Her hot tongue explored his teeth and then his mouth. In her eagerness, she pulled hard on his root.

"Can I shave first?" he asked, looking into her anxious eyes.

"No." She shook her head. "I can't wait another minute."

"All right. Give me the towel." He stood up and water went all over. He looked down, considered the consequences of his spillage, and laughed as he rubbed himself dry. "Folks in the bar'll think it's raining outside and the roof leaks."

She smiled back, seated cross-legged in the middle of the bed waiting for him.

"Well, ain't this a fine old lumpy bed," he said, crawling on his knees across it to reach her outstretched arms.

"A wonderful bed—" Her words were cut off by his mouth, and she sprawled on her back under him.

His hands moving over her rock-hard nipple and breast, they kissed their way into a hot passionate fire. She wiggled to be beneath him, and he raised up to allow her under him. She raised her slender legs and knees and sought his wand with her small hand. She inserted the head of his engorged dick in her lubricated gates, and then threw her arms back with a sigh. "Now."

His hips arched and he discovered the restraining ring inside her. She hunched her hips toward him to help, and the third time he tried, he entered the constraining circle.

She cried out and clutched him. "Oh, yes. Oh, yes."

They were lost in a whirlpool of need and spellbinding pleasure. Her legs wrapped around him and she humped against his every thrust. Her head tossing on the pillow and her moaning only added to the excitement. It could go on and on forever.

His heart pounded against his ribs. His wind grew shorter. He scrambled on his knees to keep getting into her as deep as he could. The sharp nail of her clit dragged over his sensitive shaft with each effort—then he began to realize the end was near. Both of his legs were cramping, and the explosion in his testicles flew out the end of his cannon in one last drive.

She fainted, and he had to stiffen his arms to keep from crushing her. He rolled off to the side. His eyelids weighed a ton as he hugged her small form to him. He drifted off in sleep.

When he half-opened his eyes, she was rolling him over on his back and climbing to straddle him. She inserted his half-erect dick in herself and slid down on it. Then she sprawled on top of him and whispered in his ear, "Hyrum, no matter how hard he tried, never got past that ring. Oh, Slocum, it felt so good."

He mumbled something to her, hugged her, and started back to sleep, half-dreaming of himself, Red, a packhorse, and her going to Mexico.

In the predawn, he shaved at the dresser mirror. She sat on the high-back chair and watched him.

"I want you to cut my hair," she said. "Short."

He looked back at her. "I don't have any shears."

"You can do it with your razor."

Ready to slice another soapy swath, he paused and frowned at her.

"No problem. I don't want to be bald. Just cut it off short."

"Why?" He turned back to shave.

"Because in a man's pants and shirt and with short hair, I won't be a distraction hanging around with you."

He studied the notion and swirled the blade in the pan to remove the foam and whiskers. "You're sure?"

"Yes, this dress is not the clothes to wear riding in the

saddle. I know that well. Second, I figured the less distraction I am to anyone, the easier it will be for you to take me along."

"That could be so." He watched close in the mirror as he shaved away from his ear.

"Good. Let's find the clothes after my haircut." She gathered the sheet off the bed. "This will keep the hair off me."

He rinsed the soap off the razor and shook his head. "I hope to hell you know what you're getting yourself into. It's liable to be really bad down there."

"Do I look like a coward to you?"

"No, ma'am."

"I can shoot a pistol."

"Oh."

Her blue eyes narrowed to slits. "Today, I'll show you how good a shot I am."

"Where did you learn how to shoot?" He finished washing the extra soap off his face.

"My father taught me."

"Good."

"You'll see. I can tell you don't think this little girl can shoot. But I can."

Slocum shrugged. "Let's get breakfast—your new clothes."

"After you cut my hair."

"I may slice your ear off."

She tied the sheet around her throat and took a seat as she spread the long sheet out to cover herself. "You may start."

He took a pinch of hair and sliced it off.

"Slocum. You will have to take more in your hand to ever get done."

"Yes, ma'am." Then he bent over and kissed her. When he straightened, he began to slice away at her curls by the fistful. "I have roached several mules in my day."

"Never a claybank one, I bet." She laughed.

"No, they sure weren't your color. Only saw one or two

of them in my whole life." Her hair was fast becoming much shorter under his effort.

He finished under her direction while she stood in front of the mirror. Then he pulled back and looked. She'd make a boy in the right kind of clothes. But he noticed her chewing on her lip a lot as he put up the razor.

"You regretting this deal?"

"No."

"Then why the long face?"

"I'm still a woman."

He hugged her shoulder and put his head against hers. "I ain't forgetting it."

"Just so you don't."

The young store clerk took one look at her when she asked for canvas pants and said, "My, ma'am, you'll sure take little britches."

In boy-sized underwear, denim waist overalls, suspenders, and a long-sleeve pullover blue shirt, she took on a new image. They rummaged through the store's boot stock for a pair to fit her, and they finally found some square-toed black ones with high vamps that fit over her wool socks.

Slocum selected a new .38-caliber Colt from the glass case for her, and a new cartridge belt and holster that they had to cut down to fit her narrow waist. Then, while he and the fresh-faced clerk filled the loops with new ammo, she tried on new hats. Finding a good lightweight straw, she slid the chin strap up and posed in the mirror.

"How does it look?" she said.

"Fine," Slocum said, loading the pistol and not looking up.

"I'm over here."

"Oh." He glanced at her and nodded. "You look swell."

"What's missing?" She made a face in the mirror.

Slocum walked over and took a gray silk scarf off the rack. He fitted it around her neck and held out his hand for the clerk to give him the silver ring. He drew the kerchief's tail through the ring, tightened it, and nodded. "Now look."

"Yes. Thank you." She admired the addition.

He handed her the gun belt to strap on. "Now that should complete your outfit. Wait—she needs a knife in a sheath on that thing."

The clerk handed him a small antler-handled knife in a sheath. "Here," Slocum said, and slipped it on the belt, then passed gun rig to her. "Now you look ready."

She smiled and nodded while strapping it on.

"I must warn you, there is a gun ordinance in Tombstone these days," the clerk said.

"We won't be here long," Slocum assured him.

"Fine. They do enforce it."

"I can understand why. Silver, if you're ready, let's go get the horses. This young man will help us load the packhorse when we ride back up here."

"Oh, certainly, sir."

"Thank you," she said, and smiled at him. "You have been most helpful."

"My first time." His face turned a little red.

"What's that?"

"First time I ever turned a lady into a boy."

They all laughed.

Twenty minutes later, they were loading the panniers with their needs and supplies on the packhorse. A young marshal was picking his teeth, looking them over with his shoulder against a post.

"Guess you two boys know we got us a gun ordinance in this town."

Silver looked at Slocum and they nodded at each other. Slocum turned and spoke to the lawman. "We're leaving."

"Yeah, but wearing a gun in the city limits is against the law."

"I think you heard me. We're leaving town. Right now." Silver mounted her horse and he did his.

The marshal threw down his toothpick. "See you obey the law next time."

They were hardly thirty feet down the street when the young store clerk lit into the lawman. "Wylie, you are plumb stupid. That wasn't no boy with him, that was a lady."

"Huh? A lady?"

"I give up on you."

Down the street, Slocum winked at her. "Little Britches, you had him fooled."

9

Mexico was a faint line in the sand. The two of them crossed the border and headed southwesterly. It was a dry land of cactus, greasewood, bunchgrass, and purple saw-tooth mountains. Heat waves distorted Slocum's vision of the horizon, but his partner looked fresh in her new uniform. Their horses were rested as well and held a good trot.

At mid-morning, they stopped at a small well beside the dim road they traveled, and drew water for the horses and themselves. While he pulled up water for the horses, she found some discarded brown bottles and stood them up on the far bank of the arroyo.

When she climbed out, she pushed the new hat to the back of her head. "Now, Slocum, watch this."

She drew the small handgun, cocked it, took aim, and fired. The glass bottle busted into shards, and Slocum spoke to the startled packhorse. "Go ahead," he said to her, holding the packhorse firmly.

Numbers two and three went to fragments, she busted a piece off the top of the next one, and smashed the last one. Her gun hand dropped to her side and she turned slowly to face him.

"Well?"

He took off his hat and scratched his head. "Why, you're plumb full of surprises, Little Britches."

She gave him a smug nod and holstered the gun.

He reset the hat and handed her the reins to her horse. "All right, don't forget to reload it."

In the saddle, she nodded. "All right."

"Shooting a man ain't like shooting a bottle, but if it's your life or his, you learn how," he said, and booted Red out in a trot. Maybe she'd learn that. He hoped she never needed to, but where they were going anything could happen. And probably would.

That evening, he bought them food from a woman vending in the street of Enterado, a dried-up village at the base of the Madres. The hot and spicy meat-bean burritos were wrapped in fresh-made blanket-size flour tortillas. He nodded to her as they squatted beside the adobe wall in the twilight. "What do you think now?"

"Woo, that's hot!" she said.

"You'll get used to it."

With her free hand, she fanned her mouth, then she winked at him. "I'll be fine."

He spun on his toe at the sound of a horse coming down the street. The vaquero came by ignoring them. A gun butt stuck out of his holster in the dimming light. By the grade of the fine horse he rode, there was no doubt he was a pistolero. Many haciendas kept pistoleros on their payroll. They were peacekeepers, assassins, and the final resolvers of any problem the *patrón* needed taken care of.

"You know him?" she asked, no doubt seeing Slocum's obvious interest in the rider.

"No. I wondered why he's here." He turned to the old woman and spoke in Spanish. "You know him?"

She shook her head. "Never see him here before."

"Gracias."

"What do we do now?" she asked.

He rubbed his upper lip as he cupped his mouth in consideration. "If he's out of work, we could use him."

"How will you find that out?"

"Go ask him." He looked off down the street at the silhouette of the barb horse standing at the hitch rail. The animal's dish face and small pin ears were on alert in the light coming from behind the batwing doors.

"Isn't that dangerous?"

"Ain't much in this land won't sting or bite you."

She handed him the last of her burrito for him to eat. "I'm ready."

"I was thinking you could tend the horses."

"I'm with you, big man."

"All right, Little Britches."

She held her hand out to stop him. "I like Little Britches much better than ma'am."

He nodded.

They led their horses down the caliche street and hitched them beside the barb. Slocum shifted the Colt on his hip, nodded to her, and led the way through the creaking batwing doors. Once inside in the flickering candlelight, he motioned her toward a booth. She slid in first.

The bartender came over.

"Dos cervezas," Slocum ordered.

The man nodded. Slocum motioned for him to come closer. "If that hombre standing at the bar needs work, send him over."

"Ah, Señor," the man whispered. "He must be a pistolero."

"I know. Do it."

The bartender went for their beers, and Slocum watched him tell the man. The vaquero looked over in his direction and Slocum nodded.

The barkeep rushed over, set down their beers, and left as if he was scared.

"Here he comes," she whispered, pulling the mug toward her side.

The vaquero carried his glass over and stopped, standing above them.

"Slocum is my name. That's Little Britches."

"My name is Vegas." He tossed down some mescal from

the glass, but made no move to join them. "What work do you have for me?"

"Pays fifty American."

"What must I do?" He shifted his weight to his other boot and the spur rowel rang.

"Be sure the gold train gets through."

"You have a mine?"

"The one I work for has the mine."

"There must be *bandidos*." The man looked reflectively at the finger of mescal left in his glass.

"You know Henry St. John?"

"I have heard of him."

"Scare you?"

"No. Where do you go now?"

"In the morning we ride to the mine."

He closed his left eye to stare hard at Slocum out of his right one. "Why does he have a gringo in charge for his security?"

"Not a he. They killed her husband. Have a seat. Your glass is empty. I'll buy you a good bottle. We can talk of the men we know."

The man swept off the heavy sombrero and hung it on a hook. Then he scooted into the opposite bench and looked hard at Little Britches. "What do you do for this woman?"

"Whatever she needs."

Vegas chuckled in his throat at his discovery. "A woman disguised as a man. I wondered who you were."

"She's not the point," Slocum said. "Lucia Valenta is the woman I work for."

"Oh, my, yes. She is some woman. I have seen her at the hacienda. They killed her husband?" He spread his hands out on the table. His wrists were wrapped in stiff cuffs. His dusty leather clothing fit him well. A silver cross swung from around his neck.

"A short while ago, she asked me to return and help her. I quit him three weeks ago because I told him he needed to hire more guns to protect his interests and he refused my request."

"And got himself killed?"

Slocum nodded. "Where have you worked?"

"I was born on the Aquares Hacienda. Like all good children, I grew up there, learned all the skills that I have there. But the *patrón* died a year ago and the senõra remarried—this man she married had his own pistoleros. She called me to the house and paid me in gold. She gave me the fine horse and she hugged me. Then she told me I must leave.

"I left, but there was no work for a pistolero wherever I stopped."

"Where were you going tonight?" Slocum asked.

A slow smile spread over his handsome face. "To look for work." He nodded toward the mountains. "They said Henry St. John would hire me."

"Oh, damn . . ." Silver sucked in her breath.

10

The three of them rode alongside the noisy rushing stream. Giant gnarled cottonwoods followed its course. The air was cooler and junipers dotted the hillsides above them. At midday, they took a meal break in a small village. On the narrow street, they found an old woman selling meals and she made them corn tortillas filled with some meat and sauce.

Her face was as wrinkled as a dried whole apple and she talked nonstop.

"Where do you go?" she asked.

"To see some amigos in the mountains."

"Hmm." She sniffed. "Two pistoleros and a young boy. I know where you go."

"Where is that?" Slocum asked, not listening to half the things she said.

"Ha. You go to Valenta's mine where the friends of Mexico's poor people have taken over the mine."

Slocum frowned at her words. Mexican poor people have the mine? "When did they do that?"

"Maybe two weeks ago. They are in charge and will share the riches of the mountains with workers now that they have it."

"Who says they will share it?" Slocum asked.

"St. John. He told everyone when he got in charge he would share it with all the people."

"What have they done to the señora?"

The old woman cackled. "They have shipped her ass to Mexico City. Sold her pussy to the slave market. I hope lots of dirty stinking dicks poke her cunt every night."

"You know this to be the truth?"

"They brought her by here two days ago."

"Who?"

"A man called Freddie Fine. He and some horny pistoleros were taking her to Mexico City."

"You know this to be so?"

She cackled some more. "I saw the one they called Tigre stick his dick in her ass right here in the street. She cried and I laughed. That bitch beat her last maid."

"She beat you?" Slocum asked.

"No, but she beat my cousin."

"What for?"

"She said she stole jewelry."

"How much did she sell the jewelry for?"

"Not enough for the beating she got."

He simply nodded.

When they left the old woman and went to water their horses at the stream, Slocum looked back. "We must see if we can get her away from Freddie Fine. Vegas, you know this man called Tigre?"

"He is a mean man who cares for no one. Who is this Freddie?"

"A worthless gunrunner who makes slaves out of women."

"I wonder who is the other pistolero," Vegas said.

"We'll find out. We must go after them."

"Can the three of us handle them?" Silver asked.

"Sure." Slocum wasn't worried about those three men being any threat to them. The treatment of poor Lucia at their hands before he found her worried him much more. Tigre screwed her in the street—he shuddered at the thought.

They pushed their horses southwestward to clear the mountains. Vegas knew some shortcuts so by the time they made camp late after sundown, Slocum felt they were making progress and in another day of hard pushing they should catch up with Lucia Valenta's captors.

"Maybe at Norte," Vegas said. "We can catch them there."

Slocum agreed. There were many cantinas and things available for them at the town. The liquor, *putas,* and food would be easier to find there. They might even have to rest there.

"You are upset over this kidnapping?" Silver asked him later that night in their bedroll. She was snuggled against him, and her warm skin felt good pressed to his own under the covers as the temperature dropped.

"Lucia was never mean to her help. I have been around her. That woman's cousin stole from her."

She chuckled. "What did she say? She didn't get enough for the beating she got?"

He shook his head at the thought of what the woman said. "And St. John won't share a damn thing with those people."

She nested her rock-hard breasts in his chest. "I hope we find her."

"Oh, we will find her. Trust me." He hoped it was not too late.

"Where is that boy who brought you the message from her?"

"Largo? I don't know. He's brave, but he's also young and inexperienced."

She reached underneath her stomach and pulled on his tool. "Make me forget all the bad things."

"I hope that's that easy." He raised up and kissed her.

They were soon caught in a tornado of passion. His thoughts were whirling like a spinning twenty-dollar gold piece on a bar top as he sought her depths with a burning-headed erection and his needs screamed at him. Then the passion died and they slept in each other's arms.

At dawn, they ate a beef jerky breakfast and hurried on. At mid-afternoon, they reached the outskirts of Norte. An old man with an oxcart who they met on the road had seen

Lucia and her captors that morning riding into Norte. Slocum paid him two bits and the man grinned, swept off his hat, bowed, and thanked him.

"Will they stop in Norte?" Silver asked when they rode on.

Vegas nodded. "They have no boss with them, huh? And there are many things which they have in this town where they can spend any money they have."

"Where will we start looking for them?" she asked.

"We'll make camp and go into town after dark. They may know me," Slocum said.

Vegas shrugged and laughed. "They don't know me. I will go look for them."

Slocum agreed. "Be careful and come get me if you locate them."

Later, as Slocum sat on his butt in camp, time ticked very slowly. The sun crawled across the sky to die in the distant Gulf of California. Red flares of the impending solar funeral at last signaled night was coming.

Little Britchas hurried over, bringing him a plate of frijoles and tortillas bought earlier. Vegas had not returned, which meant he was still looking or was busy sizing up the situation. Slocum thanked her absently and began to eat. His appetite was numbed by his concern for Lucia in the hands of those bastards.

At the sound of a horse coming, Silver stood up. "Vegas is coming back."

"Good." He handed her his plate and went to meet the man.

"They are in this village," Vegas said, dismounting heavily. "They are staying at a fancy house. The woman is with them."

"Whose house?"

"Some old *general* named Matteras."

Slocum whistled. "Cotteral Matteras."

"Who is he?" Vegas asked.

"They use to call him the Butcher of Sonora. He poisoned Apaches at parties he hosted for them. He shipped all the mine workers that struck the Cantilena Mine off to the Yucatan and sold their wives and daughters into slavery. On the Yaqui River, he shot all the male squatters and his army raped the rest."

"Nice guy. Why would they stop there?" Silver asked.

"He probably has a cell to hold her in while they raise hell in town."

"What do we do next?" she asked, busy filling a plate of food for Vegas.

"We'll go see if we can get her out."

"He has guards," Vegas said. *"Gracias."* He took the tin plate piled high with beans and tortillas from her.

"I bet no one has challenged them in years," Slocum said. "A sentry force like that gets laggard, especially in Mexico."

"You better eat. You'll need all the strength you can find to get her out of there, I'd bet," she said.

Slocum laughed. "Yes, Mother. Vegas, tell us more about the place."

"It has high walls and armed guards at the gate. I went on a nearby hill and discovered there are several buildings inside besides the large casa."

"Maybe we should wait till they bring her out?" she asked.

"Have you never breached a castle before?" Slocum asked her, picking up his plate and sitting back down on the ground to finish his meal.

"Oh, yes, many times," she said.

They all laughed.

Later, in the dark, they crouched in the night near the compound wall. Slocum had discovered a weak link in the chain. An old gate left unlocked.

"I am certain we can get it open and slip inside."

"Then what?" Vegas asked, squatted on his heels with them.

"Then we storm the castle."

The man nodded.

"What should I do?" she asked.

"Bring the horses on the run when we come out with her."

"What if you don't find her in there or they capture you?"

"Then we go to our next plan."

"What is that?"

"I haven't figured it out yet."

She laughed. "I'll be ready. When do I give up on you getting out?"

"Sunup and we aren't out, you draw back and go home."

"Are you serious?"

He looked hard at her. "Dead serious. We aren't out of there by sunup, you go home."

She twisted around to look at Vegas, who affirmed Slocum's words with a sharp nod. Then she shook her head in dismay. "You two are crazy."

Slocum nodded. They were, but he knew no better way to rescue the lady. He owed her that much. Somehow, in the next few hours, they needed to get Lucia out of there and be gone.

"How will you signal me?" she asked when they dismounted in a dry wash above the general's palace.

"Get back up the hill and watch for us to come out the gate. Then bring those horses on a dead run."

She nodded. "I really am worried."

He kissed her and then rose. "So are we."

Vegas nodded at her. *"Vayas con Dios."*

"You two will need God's help worse than I do."

They left her and hurried under the stars toward the gate on a path through the cactus and the greasewood brush. Slocum lifted the latch, and the walk-in door built in the gate opened on creaky hinges. Inside, they both crouched for a moment to get their bearings. Then Slocum indicated the lighted house and they headed for it.

They heard the chatter of women talking in the kitchen, and skirted to a pair of dark French doors. Slocum tried the latch and it opened. Both men slipped inside. The room contained a large bed that the light from outside shone on.

The walls were covered with volumes of books in book-cases. He decided it was a library and guest room.

At the door, he listened, heard nothing, and opened it. The hall's small candle lamps shed an orange glow as the two men eased out and headed for the front of the house. Footsteps coming made them slip into a dark room. At the cracked door, Slocum could see it was a waiter returning with a tray. He stepped out and coughed.

The man turned and frowned at the .44 in his face. With his gun muzzle, Slocum waved the man into the room. "No tricks or you die."

"Who—who are you?"

"Hush. Where is Señora Valenta, the woman they brought in today?"

"I know nothing—"

Vegas laid his knife's edge at the man's throat. "You have only minutes left in your miserable life. Where is she?"

"Top of the stairs in the first bedroom."

"Tied up?"

He shook his head. "No, she is having a Chinese dream."

"Opium."

Vegas returned Slocum's stern nod.

"We're going to tie you up and gag you," Vegas said in the man's ear, and began to bind his hands behind his back. "You make one sound, we'll come back and cut your throat."

"I won't. I swear."

"Your life depends on it, amigo," Slocum said.

"How do we get upstairs?" Vegas asked the trembling waiter.

"There are stairs in the back of the house."

Slocum gave Vegas a nod. When the man was securely bound and gagged, they slipped outside again and worked their way around. Time was sand in an hourglass, drizzling away. The fact they had Lucia doped made Slocum upset. It meant carrying her out of there, and she would be unable to help them or herself. They slipped in through a rear door. The women were wrapping up their work and leaving the kitchen. Slocum and Vegas squatted behind a wall and waited as the women's voices trailed off into the night.

In the kitchen that they entered, it smelled of cooking odors, with garlic and onions. They moved across the dimly lighted area, and found the door to the dark staircase that the waiter had promised. At the head of the stairs, Slocum put his ear to the door and listened. He heard voices that he suspected were in the lower part of the house.

He turned the knob, opened the door, and eased onto the second-floor balcony, which was fenced by a railing. Vegas joined him. They stayed close to the wall, hoping no one saw them, and moved toward the door Slocum hoped was Lucia's room.

He turned back and nodded to Vegas, who held his pistol close to his face ready for anything. They exchanged a look of satisfaction and started on again. The creak of the floor sounded like a scream and made them stop.

At last, Slocum opened the door and eased inside. Vegas quietly closed the door. Slocum went over by the bed where the soft lamplight shone on Lucia's ashen face. The thought of how these perverts had used her body made him angry and sick to his stomach. She slept, or was passed out.

"Lucia, Lucia, wake up."

She mumbled. "What?"

"It's me, Slocum. Can you wake up?"

"Nooo."

"I'm getting you out of here," he said, taking the covers back and seeing she was in a thin negligee. He swept her up in his arms and nodded to Vegas. "Let's go."

"Sí," the man said with a grim look written on his face in the flickering light.

Slocum shifted her in his arms. All they had to do was get downstairs, across the yard, through the gate, and signal for Silver to bring the horses. A long ways to go, but with luck—they'd need it. They went back the balcony, and Vegas led the way to the entrance to the back staircase.

Voices and laughter from below filtered up to them from the main hall. Vegas opened the door and let Slocum, with

Lucia in his arms, into the dark hallway. Step by step, he descended the stairs. He shifted his load and she moaned softly.

"It's okay. We're getting you out of this hell," he whispered.

At the foot of the stairs, he unlocked the door, boosted her in his arms, and stepped into the kitchen.

"Where are you going with her?" a voice demanded.

Slocum turned to face a large man holding a pistol on him. "Going for some air. It was stuffy in there."

"You make joke?"

"No—"

Vegas came out of the door to the staircase and shot the man. The lamp went out from the percussion of the shot. Acrid gun smoke boiled up in the room. The big man crumpled and Slocum headed for the rear door with Lucia in his arms.

He could hear the shouting, and hoped the gunshot would signal Little Britches to come at once. Vegas ran beside him across the open yard toward the side gate. "I couldn't think what else to do."

"You did—" Slocum caught his breath. "You did wonderful."

"They are coming."

"Shoot whoever you have to." His legs and arms ached, but he found some new strength.

At last, they were at the gate. Shots began to thump into the wooden gate as Slocum ducked, opened it, and went through. Once outside, he looked back, relieved that Vegas had secured it closed. The sound of hoofbeats coming down the arroyo made his hard-beating heart slow a little, and Little Britches shouting to the horses made him feel some comfort.

Vegas rushed out to catch his horse. He bounded into the saddle, and Slocum handed him the limp Lucia. He took her and his barb lunged away in the night. Half aboard his own saddle in the starlight, Slocum saw the gate burst open and a face appeared.

He shouted for Silver to run and drew his Colt. Shooting across his own body, he slung lead at the gate. There were shouts from someone hit and then as Red tore out, Slocum's six-gun clicked on empty. All he could do was holster it and urge the stout mountain horse away.

With the drum of Red's hoofbeats under him, he chased the fleeing figures of Silver and Vegas ahead of him. His breath came in shorter gasps as he tried to fill his aching lungs. There would be pursuit. But for now they were free. Staying free was what might be tricky.

11

By sunup, they had recovered their packhorse and were headed into the Madres. Vegas knew of a place where he felt they could hide out for a while in the mountains' vastness. The rescued Lucia was hardly coherent, and Vegas carried her in his arms like a large doll. Slocum sent the three of them on while he dropped back and checked on their back trail for any sign of pursuit.

On his stomach scanning the country for a sign of dust, he found nothing in his scope, and soon caught and mounted Red to catch up with them. He hoped that they could soon find a place to rest. His eyes were dry and sore from lack of sleep. A few hours' rest, if they could risk it, might freshen all of them. The mountain horse cat-hopped up the steep-sided slope, and he was soon on another flat racing to catch up.

They stopped beside a spring that fed a small stream, green with watercress. The pure water flowed out of a large hole in the rock. Slocum bellied down and soaked his face.

Little Britches sat on her butt and rested her forehead on her knees. Still drugged, Lucia slept on a blanket on the ground close by. Vegas squatted on his heels and smoked a corn-husk cigarette.

"I knew when that hombre spoke to you in the kitchen

we were caught," Vegas said. "It didn't do my heart any good."

Slocum dried his refreshed face on his kerchief. "Little Britches, you all right?"

She looked up and then nodded woodenly. "Fine. I think now that we're up here, it all kinda caught up with me."

Slocum agreed and rose. He walked over to look at the sleeping Lucia. Maybe the drugs would soon wear off. No telling what they had given her. A wonder they hadn't killed her. That lousy St. John had made much worse plans for her than murdering her. He simply had hired some slovenly careless jerks in Freddie Fine and Tigre.

Silver came over and hugged his arm, looking down at Lucia. "Will she be all right?"

"She's a very strong person. But she's been through hell."

"Is there anything we can do for her?"

"I think by the time we get to where we are going to camp tonight, the drugs they gave her should be wearing off."

"She's very pretty."

Slocum nodded and scooped Lucia up. He handed her to Vegas, who was on horseback, and laughed. "Tough job, but someone has to do it."

"Ah, toughest job in my life." The row of his even white teeth showed his pride in being allocated the job of transporting her.

They all laughed, and Slocum ran for his horse.

They rode single file up the confines of the deep canyon. The high-water marks showed signs of flash floods, with driftwood and debris from past floods lodged in place over their heads. The sound of horseshoes striking hard rocks echoed off the canyon walls. Slocum kept looking at the dizzying heights above and the circling vulture. He hoped the black bird didn't know something that Slocum didn't.

The temperature rose in the confinement of the stone walls. Some scant vegetation clung to the meager dirt on the ground. As they climbed higher, a breeze funneled down the canyon, and Slocum winked at Little Britches.

"We may live yet."

"Whew, it is cooler up here." She looked over at him. "I think Vegas is talking to her."

"Good."

"Will they find us up here?"

"Who knows? They won't want her alive bringing the authorities down on them for stealing her mine. I have figured some of their plan out. If they had nobody to say she died, then her heirs don't get the mine. No one can argue that she didn't leave St. John in charge."

"So how do we get the authorities to do something about him?"

"Get her well enough to meet with them."

"Oh, this all sounds so complicated."

Vegas turned his horse back and rode alongside of Slocum. "He is here," he said to the woman in his arms.

"I-I can't thank you enough—"

"Save your strength, Lucia. We can talk more later."

"But all of you are such brave people. I know you carried me out and they were shooting. Oh, I could do nothing. It wasn't a dream, was it?"

"No. Señora, it was real and he carried you a long ways," said Vegas.

Lucia nodded and fell asleep again.

"Vegas, you tired of holding her?" An eagle screamed above them and distracted Slocum. He smiled as the dark-colored bird of prey challenged them again from on high.

"No, no, I would ride to the end of the earth holding her in my arms," said Vegas.

"Fine." Slocum winked at Little Britches. "I'll let you."

That evening, Slocum gave Lucia his extra shirt to wear. The tail came almost to her knees, and she laughed. "Ah, it is a little short, but better than nothing."

Lucia and Little Britches struck up a conversation that went on and on. The men made firewood and stayed away.

Seeing Lucia behaving almost normally with Little Britches made Slocum feel a lot better. They were camped for the night in the pines, a day's ride from the hideout Vegas had proposed.

While they ate their beans, Slocum asked Lucia who else was with her captors besides Freddie Fine and El Tigre.

"A man they called Juarez. I never heard him called anything else."

Slocum nodded. "Vegas, you know that one?"

He shook his head. "I know Tigre because he came by the hacienda once to seek help finding a man he said stole some horses from his *patrón*."

"Was that true?"

"I think the man double-crossed him on the horse deal and took the horses on to sell them in El Paso."

Lucia closed her eyes and spoke through her teeth. "If I ever get a chance, I'll blow his balls off." She shuddered and dropped her chin.

"Lucia? Lucia?" Slocum said to get her attention. "We're going to get your mine back and settle with them."

"Oh, Slocum, I know that—"

"We'll do it."

She looked up at them with wet lashes. "They have killed so many."

"Tell us about someone we can trust in the government."

She shrugged and turned her hands up. "I don't know who to trust."

"Vegas, Little Britches, and me for one."

She tried to smile. "I had prayed and prayed and when you came for me, I knew God had sent you."

Vegas was on his knees holding her against his chest. "Señora, you will be safe with us."

She pushed him back so she could peer into his face. "Vegas, my name is Lucia. Call me that, please?"

He hugged her tight and rocked her in his arms. "Lucia. Lucia. We will care for you."

"What should we do?" Little Britches asked Slocum.

"First, we must find an official we can trust."

"Is the *general* you took her from in with them?"

"If he isn't, he's getting paid to keep the real officials away from the mine."

Silver frowned at him. "Does he have that much influence?"

"Way too much, I fear."

In the predawn, their horses were saddled and the pack-horse made ready to go as the soft purple of sunup touched the peaks above them. A shot rang out. Slocum felt the burning sting in his shoulder. It staggered him.

Little Britches screamed, "He's hit."

"Get the hell out of here," Slocum shouted, and grabbed for his left arm. The pain sent lightning chills to his cheek. "Go!"

Vegas tossed Lucia on his horse and leaped in the saddle behind her. Little Britches gave Slocum a hurt look.

"Get out of here," he screamed.

She obeyed and caught the spooked packhorse. Slocum was in the saddle and bullets were whizzing all around him. He bent over the saddle horn, his stirrups flapping, his good hand grasping the horn to stay in the saddle. Red needed no urging. He soon caught up with Little Britches and the packhorse. Behind them the shooting had silenced.

"How bad is it?" she asked as they raced side by side through the open timber.

"Don't worry. I'm still ticking."

"For how long?"

He shook his head. He was grateful that Vegas and Lucia were farther ahead of them—maybe they'd escape. "Can you see anyone back there?" he asked.

"Yes. I caught sight of something."

"Stop," he said.

"Why?"

"Stop and help me."

"Do what?" She reined up and bolted out of the saddle. Gathering reins, she moved in to help him.

"I'm—fine."

"You don't look fine. What're you doing?"

"We—got to stop them—" He jerked the rifle and stick out one-handed. "Shells in my saddlebags."

He laid the rifle over his leg and cocked it.

She had the cartridge. "Now what?"

"Open the block and put it in."

She obeyed and closed the rolling block. He released the hammer carefully and recocked it.

"Put it in the forks and hold it steady."

He looked through the telescopic sight. Slick warm blood was seeping into his shirt. Twice, he blinked to get his eyes to focus. *Don't fail me now*. Then he could see the lead rider.

"You all right?" she asked, holding the stick in one hand, the reins in the other.

"Yeah. Get ready to get another cartridge."

"I have two more."

"Good." He squeezed off a shot, and at the blast she had to let go of the stick to control the horses.

He knew the lead rider was gone. He needed one more of the four taken down. Dizzy-headed, he swung the rifle over his leg one-handed and cocked it. She opened the block, ejected the casing, and put a fresh one in.

"I have the horses tied together, they won't go far," she said.

He knew. He nodded. Could he even see one more? She put the rifle in place and held the stick in both hands for him. With the stock to his shoulder, he tried to see the other riders dodging through the trees toward them. With care, he found one in the crosshairs and shot. In the blinding smart smoke, he saw the rider throw his arms up, hit hard, and cartwheel off his horse.

"They're leaving," she shouted in his ear. "The others are turning tail and running."

He blinked. Maybe he'd stopped them—he hoped so.

"Get on the horse, Slocum, I can lead you." Her words brought him out of his dizziness.

"I'll try—"

"No! Get on that horse! Oh, damn, you're all bloody."

She put her shoulder against his butt, and he found himself in the saddle.

"Hold on. I'll lead you."

"Yeah," he said, the lights in his head going on and off.

He had no idea how far they had ridden when she began beating on his leg for him to get down. Where were they?

"Slocum. Slocum, I can help you. But I can't carry you."

"I—know." The sound of his own weak voice shocked him. He grasped the horn as he eased himself down. Oh. God—

"Slocum. Slocum. You passed out on me. Can you hear me? I want you over there in the shade."

"Sure." Couldn't walk. He could crawl. Pain in his left arm caused him to consider throwing up. "I don't think I can go over there."

"Stay here then," she said, and ran for the bedroll.

At last he was facedown—the world went black.

She woke him again. "How can I stop the damn bleeding?"

"See—see how deep the—bullet is."

"How can I do that?"

"Feel for it." Oh, damn, he could hardly stay awake.

"Feel how?"

"Small pointed knife. Get it out, then—then cauterize it."

"What is that?"

"Get some gunpowder, pour it in the wound, and set it on fire . . ."

"Oh, my God. What if I can't do that?"

He fainted again.

When he awoke, his shoulder felt on fire. She held an object between her fingers in front of him—a lead bullet. Bent over close enough for him to see it, she said, "I got the bullet out. Did it all. You have to live now."

"I'll try," he said.

"Try? No, you have to live."

It was dark when he awoke again. She rushed over when he tried to sit up. "I'll help you."

Sitting up at last, the pain in his left shoulder still cob-webbing his brain, he nodded woodenly. "Where's Vegas and Lucia?"

"I have not seen them since we rushed away. Maybe he went on to the hideout."

"It could be. Any sign of those others?"

She shook her head and sat down beside him. "Just you, me, and some old lobo wolf that's been hanging around."

"I doubt he'll bother us."

"I wish I was that sure."

"Thanks," he said, and she hugged him lightly. "Been a helluva day."

"A damn long one." She shook her head. "What else do I need to do? I reloaded your pistol, too."

"Thanks, I may need it. Wait and see is all I can think about doing right now. Keep our guns close." His six-gun and holster were wrapped in the belt close by his bedroll.

"You won't be able to travel for a few days."

"Morning we better move on."

Wrinkles of concern crossed her smooth forehead. "You're in no shape to ride anywhere. Besides, where will we go?"

"We need to try to find Vegas. I figure if he's alive, Vegas will come back when he has Lucia secure someplace."

She nodded.

"I never figured they'd jump us that soon," he said. "They really must have pushed hard to find us." The fact that they'd made that big of a push meant they didn't want Lucia to escape. Maybe they feared St. John's reaction over their loss of her. No telling.

"Did you recognize any of those men you shot?" she asked.

"No, they all looked like strangers."

"Someone is coming," she said, and sprang to her feet. The .38 Colt in her fist was cocked.

Slocum had heard the horse snort off in the timber to the south.

"Hold your fire, amigos."

"It's Vegas," she said, and reset the empty cylinder under the hammer before she holstered the handgun.

On foot, the vaquero crossed into the fire's light with a look of relief written on his bronze face. "Thank God you two are all right."

"How is Lucia?" Slocum asked.

"I have her safe with an old woman who is a doctor. Lucia had bad headaches all day. She thinks it is from all the dope they gave her." He squatted down and looked over at Slocum. "They shot you?"

"Yes. Doc here got the bullet out and stopped the bleeding." He gave a nod toward Little Britches.

Vegas drew his head back and frowned. "You are a doctor?"

She laughed at his reaction. "Today I had to be one."

"I see. What should we do now?"

"Move on in the morning," Slocum said. "I took out two of them with my rifle this morning. The other two could still be out there, or they've gone back for more help."

"I will guard you tonight," said Vegas.

"No," she said. "I can do some of it."

Vegas nodded in agreement. "I will sleep a few hours then."

"Fine."

"I'm going to sleep," Slocum said, anxious to escape his throbbing shoulder. "Be careful, both of you, these are desperate men."

Sleep came hard and his dreams were all bad. Then he awoke in the night and realized there was a tough unfamiliar voice talking in their camp.

"Listen, boy. I'm going to cut your throat. Where is that damn woman?"

Facedown, Slocum edged his hand slowly for the Colt beside him on the ground. Boy? They must have Little Britches. Where in the hell was Vegas?

"I-I don't know—"

Then there was a scream by a man.

On his knees, Slocum looked up. He could see a man

under the sombrero hugging his guts and stumbling toward him. The intruder was gasping about being killed. He dropped to his knees, and then Slocum could see he was clutching a knife in his guts.

Where was she? Then a gunshot cut the night and the big man jerked up, obviously struck in the back by a bullet. He fell belly-down on the knife and groaned.

"You all right?" she asked Slocum, out of breath, holding her pistol in both hands while standing over the man.

"Fine. Where's Vegas?" Slocum asked.

"I don't know." She dropped down beside him in tears. "There was nothing else I could do."

"I know. Are there any others?" He laid down his gun and sat back on his heels. His back throbbed. "We have to find out if there's more. That shot will bring them."

She looked around in the starlight filtering through the pines. "I don't see anyone."

"Good. We need to find Vegas."

"I'll look for him."

"I'll be behind you."

"I was asleep when that man jerked me up. When he looked around, I took the knife you gave me out of my belt and used both hands—I didn't know what else to do but shoot him."

"That must be Vegas." Slocum pointed to a prone figure on the ground.

"Oh, is he dead?"

Slocum knelt down beside the man and turned him over. Vegas gave a groan and blinked his eyes. "Who hit me?"

"I think the man she shot. You all right?"

"I have a bad headache."

"You notice anything? I mean, obviously he jumped you, too."

"Nothing. He must have been part Indian. I thought I had heard a horse down the way and got up—then the lights went out."

Slocum sat on the ground beside the recovering Vegas.

"There were four of them. I shot two. This big one makes three."

"One more is out there?" she asked, finally holstering her revolver and squatting beside him.

"Hell only knows, but my count is three down, one to go."

Vegas rubbed the back of his neck. "I'll go check on that sound of a horse I heard before he slugged me over the head."

"Better wait till you have your wits about you." His own head felt light and his shoulder was on fire.

"What will we do about—him?" she asked.

"Let the buzzards have him. He made his own fate." Slocum looked off in the night at the peaks above them. Lucia would sure be upset that they had not returned. He could only hope she was still in safe hands.

"I'll be all right." Vegas rose, and discovered his pistol was gone. "He must have gotten it."

"Here, take mine," Slocum said, and handed it to him. "I'll get yours off him."

Vegas moved off in the night. Slocum raised up on his knees, then she steadied him to stand. They walked back to the prone outlaw. He didn't move.

Slocum put out his good hand and motioned for her to give him her pistol. Even dead rattlers sometimes struck. When he had the six-gun in his hand, he nodded. "Now roll him over on his back careful-like."

On her knees, she reached over and tried to turn the big man over. With the .38 cocked and ready, Slocum watched her, wishing he was the one struggling to flop the outlaw on his back. With much grunting, she at last managed get the outlaw on his side. Then, in limp fashion, he fell on his back.

She snatched a revolver out of the man's holster and tossed it aside. Then she moved on her knees and jerked out the one stuck in his waistband.

"Must be Vegas's." She handed it to him.

"Yes, it probably is his," Slocum agreed, and slipped it

in his own holster. "Maybe when Vegas gets back, he can tell us who this one is."

"What will we do next?"

"Maybe make something to eat, then we can load up and ride out." He reached out with his good arm and hugged her shoulder. "I'm sorry. I know this has been tough on you. But you saved our lives."

He could feel the revulsion in her about the events that had happened as she quaked under the arm draped over her. "You'll make it," he said. "Sorry it had to happen."

"I—I know I'll make it." She hugged her arms as if cold. "It is just getting there that bothers me."

He closed his eyes. He owed St. John another one for what this did to her. First Lucia, now her. Damn that worthless outlaw anyway—The sound of footsteps cut off his thoughts. His hand went for his gun butt.

"Get moving," Vegas ordered, and marched into the clearing with a prisoner.

"Who've we got here?" Slocum asked, easing himself to the ground. He had lost a lot of his own strength, and the discomfort in his back made him even more restless.

"I think you know him," Vegas said. "Freddie Fine."

"Who's he?" she hissed under her breath.

"White slaver, gunrunner, whiskey peddler. Who else is with you?" Slocum asked Fine.

"Oh, no one. I swear there ain't no one and I didn't know what Tigre was up to coming up here. He said watch the horses. That's all. I thought he had diarrhea or something like that."

"Quit lying. You came for the woman, too."

Fine spread out his hands in protest. "This wasn't my deal. I swear this wasn't my deal. I got caught up in it at the mine and it was help them or get killed. Nothing I could do. I swear. You ask her. Where is she?"

"In safe hands. Now what did the old *general* back there have to do with this?"

"He-he wanted her. The señora. But he couldn't get his

pecker up when we got there, and he wanted to try her or I guess we'd been gone."

"You were taking her where?" Slocum asked, thinking about what Donada had told him about this worthless piece of shit.

"Not me. I was just going along or die."

"You can quit lying. Tigre told us before he died that you were in charge."

"He lied. I swear he lied."

"Dead men don't lie."

"Well, if I got her sold—they were going to let me live. See, that's what he meant."

"Fine, you're the lying'st bastard I've ever met. Tie him to a tree," Slocum said in disgust. "We'll use him for mountain lion bait."

"No!"

"You better hush up. They hear you screaming, they may swarm in here thinking they got a real good meal."

"I'll make us some food," Little Britches announced.

"Good," Slocum said.

Vegas moved his prisoner over to the horses and secured a rope. Then he marched him to the nearest pine and tied the protesting outlaw to the trunk. He finished by stuffing a rag in his mouth.

"That's much better," Slocum said when the vaquero rejoined him.

"That makes four." Vegas sat cross-legged on the ground.

"No rush," Slocum said. "Get her knife out of Tigre and you can have the money on him."

Vegas nodded toward Fine. "What about him?"

"We can leave him tied up there for all I care. We'll take their horses, guns, and supplies with us."

"You think they will send more men?"

"What do you think when they fire the first cannon off?"

"Lots more to come, huh?" Vegas stood up. "I'll go get their horses and things."

Slocum agreed, silently cussing his sore shoulder.

They ate breakfast at dawn. Then Slocum managed, with Little Britches helping, to get on Red. He sat for a long moment in the saddle and let the pain chills in his face evaporate. They had four saddle horses from the outlaws. Expensive remounts from the looks of them. No doubt from the general's own stables—not bronc mustang stock. Perhaps why the outlaws were able to overtake them so quickly.

Vegas rode by Fine and jerked the gag out. "Now you can signal for the *leones* to come find you."

"Don't leave me. I'll die."

Slocum read the concerned look on the face of Little Britches and shook his head at her. "He'd've done worse things to us if he'd had the chance."

She turned in the saddle. "I understand."

Vegas had the horses in line and was starting out. She brought their packhorse along, and Slocum brought up the rear. At mid-afternoon, they came to a rushing creek that fed a village with small fields of irrigated produce and alfalfa along its course.

"This is Verde," Vegas announced. "That is Madonna Perido's casa." He pointed to a white-plastered house, and their horses' hooves pounded on the hollow-sounding wooden bridge over the sparkling stream. An older woman came out and smiled at them when she saw Vegas was with them.

"How is the señora?" Little Britches asked, dismounting.

"Oh, she is getting much stronger."

"Good."

"While you put the horses up, your friends can come inside," she said to Vegas. "And who are you?"

"Silver Temple. They call me Little Britches."

"Ah, Little Britches. She called for you. I see why you have such a name." She turned to Slocum. "You must be Slocum? Lucia was worried that you might have been shot."

"He was," Little Britches said.

"She's a mighty fine doctor, too." Slocum indicated Little Britches.

"Come." Madonna adjusted the shawl over her head and took Little Britches's arm. "I have some food and some . . ." She turned back to Slocum. "Whiskey, too."

"I could use some," he said, trying to ignore his pain.

"We should rebandage that wound, too."

He'd see about that. On the way to the house, he looked at her fields and crops. "You have a fine place here."

She smiled, pleased by his words. "It is not a large hacienda, but the people and I love it here."

"Yes," he agreed, "much better than the desert climate."

"What will you do about Lucia's mine?" the older woman asked Slocum once they were under the high ceiling of the living room.

"Get it back for her."

"You say that so easily."

"You're alive," Lucia said from the upstairs balcony railing.

"I think I am." He laughed, and then she stopped at the head of the stairs.

"Vegas?"

"He's fine, too."

Lucia looked much better and more her old self as she held her skirt high and ran down the steps.

Vegas arrived, and the three of them ate Madonna's fine food and Slocum drank her whiskey. It numbed him enough that the pain in his shoulder let go. After lunch, Madonna and her two helpers redressed his shoulder and talked about the fine job Little Britches had done on his wound.

Whiskey-numb, he went off to sleep. The trip and all the strain had drained all his strength. He slept belly-down on the bed until dark.

"Did you want to eat?" Little Britches asked him, seated on the edge of the bed.

"I'm thinking on it."

"Think hard, they're ready to eat. Where did this woman get her money?" she whispered.

"I have no idea. It may be old money. Why?"

"Old money?"

"Inheritance. I don't know her."

"She must have plenty. This house is full of real artwork."

"I saw a little of it." He started to scrub his face, but the sharpness in his shoulder stopped him. "We need to stay here as long as we dare so my shoulder will heal."

Her arm slipped over his back. "Get you well, right?"

"Right. Let's go join them. Then I can bathe and shave."

"Good." She kissed him. "We can do all that."

Over supper, Slocum learned a little about Madonna's source of money. Vegas had been there before as a guard for the wife of his *patrón* when she came to see her. That was how Vegas knew about her and this place. He had chosen well. Full of her rich food and unable to lean back in his chair, Slocum listened to the bright table conversation

"Can you imagine," Little Britches said, seeing his discomfort. "He wants a bath?"

They all laughed, and Madonna arranged one for him with her kitchen help.

After his bath, Little Britches shaved him and when she finished, he felt half-alive as he looked from their apartment's open French doors on the balcony at the starlit orchards and crops.

"How will you ever get Lucia's mine back?" she asked.

"I figure that by this time the folks at the mine have St. John figured out. That he's not going to give them anything."

"And?"

He turned back. "That they can be enlisted in running him off."

"But he has many hired guns."

"I doubt that, and those kind change sides easily. He has some border ruffians and bandits."

"What do we have? Two men and two women."

She hugged him gently and nestled her face on his shirt. "Why couldn't we have had a honeymoon here?" she asked.

He wrapped his good arm around her. "What do you want to do?"

She looked up at him like he'd lost his mind. "What did you think I want to do?"

A knock on the door, and he frowned. "Yes?"

"A man came a few minutes ago to tell me about a small army that the *general* has in the foothills—maybe a day's hard ride from here," Vegas said from outside.

Slocum went to the door. "Did he see them?"

"No, a man who rode in an hour ago saw them and told the bartender in the cantina."

"You paid him?"

"Yes."

"Good. Can you lead us out of here tonight?"

"It will be a hard ride in the dark."

"We don't need to tangle with him now. Madonna does not need us here either."

"I understand. How soon?"

"Twenty minutes or so."

Vegas nodded. "I should tell the señora?"

"Yes." Slocum watched Vegas hurry out the doorway. What next? Not only St. John to mess with, but the damn general as well.

Little Britches wrinkled her nose. "There goes the fun."

He laughed. She had a right to complain. Old pistoleros to shoot. Wounds to doctor. Ride horses into the ground and no passionate tosses in the bed. Maybe it would be better later. For his part, he hoped so anyway. Damn, his shoulder hurt again.

12

Dawn caught them high in the Sierra Madres lined out in a string, riding on a narrow ledge where only eagles perched. The ring of steel horseshoes on granite was lost in the gaping space under them. Above the tree line, the gray rock looked freshly piled there, the new fractures forced upward. An altitude headache hurt his skull, and aside from seeing Mexico in the dusty haze rolled out at their feet, he would be grateful to be lower down.

Vegas apparently knew the way. The paths he took were well worn, and obviously men and animals used them, so they must lead somewhere. The four riders rested at midmorning in a small treeless park. They ate some food Madonna sent along.

"We can be in a good place by nightfall," Vegas said.

"I'll be ready," Lucia said, seated on the ground in a divided riding skirt and a blouse that Madonna had loaned her. "I am about dizzy from being so high."

"Better to be here, I guess, than facing those men," Little Britches said, squatted close by her.

"Oh, dear, I am not ungrateful, just tired."

"I think you have done well for all you've been through," Little Britches said.

"Vegas told me about the outlaw. I'm sorry you had to fight my battles."

"I don't mind. That's over. Besides, you've had enough bad deals. You need your mine and home back."

"Well—"

"Mount up," Vegas said. "We can talk later."

Slocum nodded, and felt the cool wind sweep his smooth face as he rose. A nice place at a lower altitude would be fine with him. He used his right arm to grasp the horn and remounted Red. Stiff, sore, and always tired summed up his condition.

Vegas's valley was well watered by a large spring and had plenty of horse graze. The women cooked supper.

"In two days we can be at her mine," Vegas said, squatted beside Slocum at a short distance from the fire.

"Maybe some of her people will help us run them off."

"Maybe St. John will be warned we're coming, too."

"He could be. No way for us to know up here."

"Perhaps when we get close, I can go in and find out."

"Be risky."

"Amigo, my life has been that."

Slocum nodded. He understood. But St. John might be the biggest danger Vegas'd ever gone up against. Someone needed to stop St. John. He wished he had a better plan. Between the pain and his headache, he felt as dull as a rock.

The next two days were uneventful. They rode over more summits and then wound down toward Lucia's mining operation. They camped at a good distance from the mine, and Vegas rode on to see what he could learn.

Slocum spent the rest of the day in camp cleaning and oiling firearms. In the late afternoon rain threatened, and with the two women's help he hung a couple of canvas cloths from tree to tree for shelter. The women moved the bedrolls, panniers, and saddles in under them.

"I wish I could go down there and help Vegas," Lucia said as the storm swept across the mountain toward them, growling and grunting like an angry bear.

"Not much we can do until we know what kind of a force St. John has down there."

Lucia reached over her head to stretch, accentuating her large breasts under the blouse. "I just feel so helpless."

"Time is on our side," Slocum said. "We'll figure it out."

Soon, pea-sized hail pecked at the new roof, and Little Britches smiled. "Glad we did that," she said, nodding at the canvas cloths.

"It'll probably rain a shower or two every afternoon up here," said Slocum. "It was strange we didn't have some coming over the divide."

The sun soon popped out and the thunder moved off. Everything glistened like diamonds. Lucia went to take a siesta. Slocum put up all the firearms he'd worked over, and went to take a siesta of his own until Vegas returned.

He'd barely closed his eyes when Little Britches woke him. "There is a horse coming. I hope it is Vegas."

Lying facedown, Slocum grunted in agreement and rose. His back was a little better. He was surviving. Maybe Vegas had some answers. The man dropped out of the saddle and looked around.

"Lucia's asleep," Little Britches told him with a grin, and he nodded.

"What did you learn?" Slocum asked.

"That Freddie Fine is there. I saw him, but he never saw me."

"I forgot all about the chance of him being there. What else?"

"St. John has several pistoleros. They drink a lot and gamble all day and night. Some are bandits. I recognized them. Others I don't know."

"How many are there?"

"Maybe a dozen or more. They have the miners and the people all scared to death."

"Ah, they are not sharing the wealth?" Slocum chuckled at the notion.

Vegas shook his head. "His men take any women they want in the village to bed."

"How can we take it over?"

"I am not certain. They have many men and there are only the two of us."

Slocum knew that, but there had to be a way. "We need some blasting sticks, caps, and cord. That would even us up."

"But how do we get them?" Vegas looked blank-faced.

Slocum winked at the serious-looking Little Britches, who was listening closely. "We have to steal them."

"You have a plan?" she asked.

"Go in there when it's dark and find where they store their explosives. Then we load some sticks and start throwing them."

Sleepy-eyed and pushing the hair back from her face, Lucia joined them. "I know where it is at. The explosives."

A small smile came over Vegas's dark lips as she slipped under his arm. "There is the answer, *mis amigos*."

"Good. After dark, we raid the powder box," Slocum said.

"Vegas, did you have any food?" Lucia asked. "Come, I will feed you. Have they wrecked my house?"

The two went off hugging and kissing each other. Slocum smiled—they made a good pair.

"And what do we do next?" Little Britches asked.

"Take a blanket and go somewhere private," he said softly, even though the other two were over at the small campfire and beyond their hearing.

With a mischievous twinkle in her eyes, she smiled at the notion. "You know, I was thinking the same thing."

"Good."

"I'll get one," she offered.

In minutes, they were out of the wind in the shade of some pines. She spread their blanket and he toed off his boots. She began unbuttoning the blouse, and soon pulled it off over her head. Then she wiggled the pants down, exposing her white slender legs. In a long step, she was hugging him and breathing on his chest.

"I have waited. I have been patient."

"You've been wonderful."

"Your shoulder—"

He shook his head at her and listened to the scream of an eagle floating overhead.

"What is it?" She used her hand to shade her eyes and follow the course of its flight.

"A large kind of eagle from the jungles of Central America."

"It's pretty. Black and white. Why is it here?"

"Cooler weather, I guess. It will go home when it gets cold."

"I won't worry about it then." She squeezed him hard and dropped to her knees before him. She lifted his semi-hard erection and kissed it. After a moment of hesitation, she began to purse her lips around it.

At the touch of her tongue, he felt lightning hit his brain. Her efforts made him want to fly. He pulled her away and kissed her wet mouth. "I want you."

She pulled him down by his right hand. He knelt, and she scooted down on the blanket. Her legs were wide apart, and he moved between them and smiled at her. She inserted him in her wet gates and he began to probe her. Pleasure spread through his brain like a sweeping grass fire. He closed his eyes and to savor the tight ring, he plunged through.

Her mouth opened, and she moaned and slung her head in pleasure's throes. The hunger they shared for each other grew hotter and wilder. Her small butt was raised off the blanket to meet him. Soon, she wrapped her legs around him and her bare heels beat a tattoo on his back. Both of them were huffing the thin cool air for enough oxygen. She gushed on, "Yes, yes. More. Oh, my God—"

Then he felt the ignition in his testicles. Pelvic bone to pelvic bone, he exploded inside her. Her fingernails dug into his back as she cried out in passion.

For a long while, they simply lay there—half asleep and basking in the closeness of their naked bodies.

"We better get some food," she announced, and sat up,

pulling her hair back from her face. Leaning on one hand for support and seated beside him, she looked back. "Unless?"

"Unless what?"

"Damn it, do I have to spell it?"

"How do you spell it?"

She reached over and clutched his half-mast shaft in her fist. "This is how I spell it."

He caught her chin and pulled her down to kiss her. "You win the spelling bee."

With a moan, she fell over on top of him and he lifted her up to suckle on her small rock-hard breast. His tongue rasped the button of a nipple, and she shoved it at him for more. His hand slid between her legs, and she spread them apart for him, with a smile at her discovery of his middle finger beginning to tease her hardening clit.

"Oh, don't stop . . ."

After the evening meal of frijoles, the four of them huddled for their final meeting before the raid, in the dying light of the day. Even though Slocum had passed it several times in the past, Lucia drew a map in the dirt to point out where the explosives were stored for him. It was to be his and Little Britches's job to secure the blasting sticks and needed items.

"How many men can you enlist?" Slocum asked Lucia.

"If the loyal ones are still there, I can get several."

"Good. We will need to arm the blasting sticks, but they'll be better than guns at taking the outlaws out."

Lucia nodded. "I won't have a mine anyway if I can't run them off."

"Eliminate them," Slocum said.

Hard-eyed, Vegas agreed with a sharp nod.

"Vegas, you keep her safe during all this. Little Britches and I will try to secure the blasting sticks."

Lucia rose and, like honeymooners who couldn't keep apart, she stood on her toes and kissed Vegas hard. She turned back in his embrace. "How can I ever thank you for bringing him to me?"

"Later," said Slocum. "Now I need you both sharp. Make love later. I'll meet you two in the draw if we can get the explosives. Watch out. There will be people in there that will run to St. John to get on his good side."

She and Vegas nodded in agreement and they started off.

"Can we kiss, too?" asked Little Britches.

He swept her up on his arms. "I may have spoken harshly to them, but they hardly realize there is a world around them."

"They call that love."

"That can be death in this business."

"I understand." She stood on her toes and kissed him. "I'll be with you all the way covering your back."

"No shooting unless you have to."

She agreed and they set out for the village. For them to slip up close to the powder house, they used the cover of willows along the creek. The moon would not come up till late, and they had to make their way slowly. He could see the mine and the tailing high above them in the starlight. His hope was that St. John was satisfied enough with his security to leave the shack unguarded. That would make things easier.

When he could see the powder building, he also saw the sombrero of a guard. He held her back with his arm.

"I'll get him," she said, and began to shed her boots and pants.

Slocum frowned at her. "What are you doing?"

"I'm going to lure him away from the front. We have no time to waste."

"Too dangerous." He couldn't allow her—

She shook her head. "Watch me."

Slocum held the .44 in his fist. His breath was raging. That dumb woman . . . He watched her prance out in the starlight toward the one under the sombrero. The small cups of her ass shone below the tail of her shirt in the pearl light.

"Who are you?" the guard asked in Spanish.

"I am Silvia." She crowded him. "Are you lonesome here?"

"Ah, ah, yes." He acted like he wished to escape.

"Give me your hand."

"What for?" His voice trembled.

"I want you to feel how tight I am." She was nibbling on his neck and ear.

"Why do you do this? Who are you?"

"Are you afraid to finger me?"

"*Madre de Dios, no.*"

Slocum could see him look around to be sure they were alone, and then he reached down to feel her pussy. She spread her bare legs apart for his entry, guided his hand down there, and bent toward him. Then she released her hold and put her hand on his shoulder to pull him closer to her. "Be easy."

"Oh, my, you are wonderful—"

She jerked his pistol out of his holster, shoved the muzzle into his nose, and whispered, "Get your damn finger out of me." With her thumb, she cocked the hammer back. "One word and you're dead."

"Please . . ."

"I've got him," Slocum said, and whipped off the guard's sombrero, grasped him by the collar, and forced him around behind the shed.

"I'll be right back," she said, and ran back in to the willows for her pants and boots.

"Where is St. John?" Slocum jerked the guard up close to his mouth.

"I don't know—in the office. His casa—"

"You've got one chance to live. Things are going to get tough around here. If you stay tied and gagged, I'll get you when it is over and you will live. Otherwise, you better have a fine suit."

"What for, Señor?"

"For your funeral." Slocum finished tying the man's hands behind his back. Then he gagged him with his own kerchief. "You staying here till it is over?"

The man nodded. Slocum went around to the front to meet the breathless Little Britches. "It was too damned dangerous, but it worked good this time," he said.

She shuddered, putting up her galluses. "It didn't feel good either."

He found a rock and pounded the large brass lock. It soon fell open, and he pulled out the chain securing the door. They went inside the small dark warehouse and closed the door again. With the light from a cupped match, he could read the labels on the wooden crates of blasting sticks. He could handle two of them. He blew out the match.

"What else do we need?" she whispered, colliding with his back.

"Caps and primer cords."

"Where will they be? This place smells bad."

"They use bat shit to make it."

He lit another match and discovered the cord. He handed her a roll and at last found the detonators. From the case, he gave her two hard paper boxes, then turned to go back.

"Where is Delgado?" a voice said, cutting the night.

They both held their breath. Slocum dried his gun hand on his pants and strained his ears to listen for more.

"He must be off diddling some *puta*."

"Yeah, who would steal this stuff anyway?"

"No one." Hiccup. "I think we can find that *puta* Rosa at her casa." Slocum could hear the drunken slur he'd missed earlier. "Then you can dick her from behind and she can blow on mine at the same time."

"Ah, you have a good—good idea, *mi amigo*."

"Is that all men think about?" she asked under her breath.

"No, but it is interesting."

She gave him a playful punch. When it was over, he'd show her what he meant. They slipped outside, and he carried two crates of the sticks in his good arm. She rechained the door and hung the broken lock back so it looked undisturbed. Then they hurried for the meeting place.

Vegas came to meet him, and Slocum gave him one of the boxes to tote as they churned sand going up the dry wash.

"Lucia found seven of her loyal men," Vegas said. "They act ready to help. They say they know how to arm the blasting sticks, too."

"Good," Slocum said, short of breath. "We need to work fast. We left the powder house guard tied up back there."

Slocum found the loyal men seated on the ground, and they rose at his approach. Lucia came forward.

"Antonio is the lead man," she said.

Slocum set the crate down, drew a deep breath, wiped his sweaty palm on the seat of his pants, and then shook his hand. "Antonio, we attack at once. Everyone needs to throw a loaded stick at the same time."

"*Sí,* this cord you brought, it burns at a meter a minute."

"We may need that much time. No, that's too long. Thirty seconds."

"This long will do it." Antonio showed the others the length they needed.

Vegas had pried open the box lids. Lucia handed the sticks out, and Little Britches had the cap boxes open for the men. They needed no instruction. They used their large knives to unfold the end of the waxed sticks, and Antonio passed out caps with the right length of cord crimped on them. They inserted the caps carefully in the opened tubes and then closed the ends.

Slocum used rawhide string to bind two more sticks around each of the loaded ones. "That should make them blow up big-time."

"Where do we use them?" Antonio asked.

"I understand many of the outlaws are in the cantina. I don't want the women hurt, so I will shoot into the air so they rush outside. Three of you be ready to toss the sticks in the midst of them. When any others come running to help them, toss a stick at them, savvy?"

"*Sí, señor,* we have all wished for guns to kill these *bastardos.*" Antonio brandished a loaded stick. "This will be the power to drive them out of this village and the mine."

"You ladies stay back. I don't know where St. John is at. Do any of you?"

"Earlier this evening, his man Angel forcibly took to him the young daughter of Ruben Aquirria. Her name is Anita. She is just a child," an older man said, and shook his head.

"Nothing we could do either," Antonio said.

"So he must be at Lucia's house with his new plaything?" Slocum asked.

"He's there all right. Maybe I could go up there and shove one of these up his ass," an old man said. "I would like to."

His words drew some laughs.

Slocum turned to his man. "Vegas, you take the women and you three be certain that St. John does not escape."

"We can do that," Lucia said with a grim set to her lips in the starlight.

"Give me a stick of that," Little Britches said to one of the men, and took a fused stick from him. Her teeth clenched when she said, "I'll use it on that no-account."

They laughed and told her to do it.

"You better be ready to run when you light it," Slocum said with a frown.

The men armed with shoulder bags full of explosives divided up. Antonio stationed them along the route to take out any of the reserves that might rush out to help the ones at the cantina. Vegas and the women went to Lucia's residence to take St. John.

Slocum and Antonio, along with two others, kept to the side of the street single file. A drunken pistolero came down the street singing off-key about a wild *caballo*. Slocum made the others stay in the dark shadows.

"Ah, hombre. You have a light?" Slocum stepped up to the man, who fumbled around in his pockets looking for matches until Slocum struck him over the head with his pistol. He went down like a poled steer. Then Slocum swept up the pistolero's six-gun and waved the others on.

When his men were set in place on the three sides of the cantina's front, he used the cap-and-ball pistol to blast holes in the sky. It did exactly what he thought it would. The outlaws rushed out the batwing doors, and the sparkling tails of the tossed blasting sticks lighted the street. The blasts were ear-shattering. Slocum uncovered his ears and looked quickly at the stunned outlaws all over the ground in front of the cantina. He feared there might still be some fight left in them.

"Again!" he ordered, and all it took was the time to light a fuse.

Up the street, other blasts went off. No doubt to stop the reserves. He spoke to Antonio. "Handle this, I'm going to go help Vegas."

"We can handle it, Señor." Antonio and his men rushed in and began to disarm the moaning and shaken pistoleros.

Slocum had his own pistol in his hand as he rushed for the large house. He had heard nothing. When he reached the open gates of the yard, he saw the front door was open. He never hesitated, and rushed in to the opening illuminated by the light inside.

Lucia was on her knees beside Vegas, who had his back to the wall. She held a bloody cloth to his head.

"You all right?" Slocum asked, looking around.

"They only grazed him," Lucia said, about to cry.

"Little Britches?"

"They took her prisoner."

"You can handle this." Slocum clapped her on the shoulder. "I better go find where they took her."

"Be careful," Lucia said after him.

He rushed through the house into the kitchen. On the floor, a sobbing teenage girl, naked as Eve, was sprawled in a pile. He dropped beside her on his knees and caught her by the shoulder as he recalled her name. "Anita. Was there a woman with short hair with them when they left?"

"Yes." She clutched her small budding breasts underneath her folded arms and turned her face away from him.

"Was she their prisoner?"

Numbly, she nodded.

The knowledge that they'd taken Little Britches as a prisoner slapped him hard in the face. A wide-eyed, older woman rushed into the room, and at the sight of him started to leave.

"Wait, get her a blanket," he said to stop her. "She has no clothes."

"Sí."

"Take care of her." There was no time to talk to this woman named Ruby, who was Lucia's head cook. He hurried out the rear door. He holstered his six-gun, wishing Red was closer, and rushed into the night. There were three saddled horses at the hitching post. He checked the girth, tightened it, and then swung on the tallest one at the rack.

The horse started to buck, but with no time for nonsense, Slocum held his head up and they went sideways into the night. Two ways St. John could go. One was over the Madres, then down over the eastern slope, or ride north into Apache country. The upper end of the Sierra Madres was controlled by the broncos that had tried to take Little Britches captive in the first place.

St. John was not liable to take that route unless he had the whiskey-peddling gunrunner Freddie Fine with him. Vegas mentioned he'd seen Fine in the village. Chances were good that Fine, St. John, and his henchman Angel had ridden north with him. Fine had ties to the renegades that could get them through.

Slocum rode through the night for the mountain road. He had no idea where they'd gone or where they'd taken her. *Little Britches, I'm coming,* he vowed silently.

13

Slocum faced dawn on foot, leading the sweaty, hard-breathing gelding and searching for sign. His eyes were too tired to do more than glance at the cracked shoe on one of the four sets of tracks he'd followed all night: St. John, Angel, Freddie Fine, and Little Britches. They were going north. But he had no supplies, no great rifle under his fender, and a worthless horse that was giving out. Maybe they were in the same shape as he was, but he was still several hours behind them by the signs and the scattered horse apples he'd found.

He always hated defeat, but reality had settled in on him. He needed several things to meet the enemy on this vast field of battle. Not the least his Remington rifle, stouter horses, supplies, and a tracker. He saw no sign of the four riders across the tops of the mountains or in the open spaces of grass above the timber. Not having field glasses did not help his cause at all.

He swung in the saddle and headed back to the mine. The situation he found himself in left a knot in his stomach. Little Britches didn't deserve the treatment she'd experience in their hands. At midday, he reached the mine and dropped out of the saddle in Lucia's yard. He clung to the horn until his legs were stiff enough to support him.

"Slocum, did you find her?" Lucia rushed out to hug him.

"No. How's Vegas?" He kissed her forehead and turned her toward the house.

"I have him in bed. A woman stitched his head and we gave him some laudanum. His head hurt him."

"He's not a complainer. I need some things."

"Anything. What can I do for you?"

"I need some supplies, my horse, a packhorse."

"The horses are here. I can get the supplies and a pack rig put together. What else do you need?"

"An Indian tracker. There was one worked here before."

"There was a Yaqui that worked here. I will check on him for you. He was a good tracker." She hooked her arm in his. "You need food, a bath, and maybe recreation?"

"Food, bath, and sleep mainly."

"Oh, I know you too well. I will send Kalia up to help you. She is *muy buena*." Her elbow nudged him. "Stop worrying, you will find Little Britches. You found me."

"I hate coming back empty-handed. Those bastards will hurt her."

"I know about that." She shook her head, and once they were inside the vestibule, she shouted for someone.

"I need food and wine for this man."

Smiling faces from all over appeared in doorways and on the second-story balcony to see who he was.

"This is the man who saved us from the *bandidos*. His name is Slocum. Get him anything he needs or wants. Where is Kalia?"

"Here, Señora." She came floating down the stairs. She was ample-breasted, and her willowy figure flowed rather than walked. She tossed the wavy dark hair back from her face and looked hard at him.

"Señor?"

"Slocum," he said, and removed his hat. "Lucia says you are very competent."

A wicked wink, and she nodded with a pouty set to her brown lips. "I will see you do not lack for anything."

"Good." He put on his hat and hooked arms with her.

"Food and wine is first." She took him away from Lucia and pointed him toward the kitchen. "You don't need to eat in the great hall, do you?"

"No, the kitchen is fine."

"Ah, a hungry man. I know all about them."

"I'll tell Vegas when he wakes up that you are safe," Lucia said. "He is very worried about you."

Slocum stopped and swung Kalia around. "*Gracias,* Lucia. Tell him he's in charge."

"Ha, he has headache so bad he can hardly see."

"He'll see good enough in the morning."

"And you will be gone?"

"Get me that tracker so I can be."

Lucia made a shooing motion with her hands. "Kalia, take that bossy gringo out of here and feed him."

"*Sí, señora.*" And she did. Her words drew a titter of laughter from the unseen house workers.

Seated on a high stool, Slocum feasted on freshly cooked lamb ribs and chops. Browned over a mesquite fire, they made his mouth water. Fresh flour tortillas with pulled beef, goat cheese, and frijoles followed. He ate like a king while Kalia refilled the red wine in his cup and shoved her firm breast into his upper arm.

He wiped his greasy mouth on a towel she handed him and grinned over at her. "Part one complete."

"They have more meat," Kalia said.

"I'm ready for a bath." He reached over his head to stretch.

Kalia clapped her hands. "Hot water in his room."

The maids scurried about the kitchen. Soon, the room was filled with steam as buckets of hot water were secured and carried off down the hall. Kalia guided him after the water bearers. Others scooted by them sideways with a bucket in each hand to get past.

A large familiar copper tub sat on the orange tile floor in the midst of a room he had not seen before. Water was poured in under her direction, and tempered with some cooler water. Satisfied, she herded all of them out.

At the door, she turned back, smiled, and then took the red blouse off over her head. The long bare breasts shook and she gave her hair a toss back while undoing the strings that held the waist of her skirt.

He toed off his boots as she threaded all her long dark hair on her right shoulder and slithered across the tile to him. She undid his gun belt and relatched the buckle to hang it on the top post of the ladder-back chair. With a grin, he noted her fine-looking hard ass. Undoing his shirt, he handed it to her, and then his pants.

She took them from him and held them while she admired his privates. She had a pensive smirk on her face. "I see why she liked you so well."

"Really?"

"We are like sisters, Lucia and I. Are you mad that she has forsaken you for Vegas?"

"No, she will need him when I'm long gone."

"Oh, yes. Stay right there while I throw these dirty clothes in the hall so they can be washed."

"Sure." He smiled when she held two fingers to her lips to make a loud whistle, then tossed the clothes out the partially open door.

"Now where were we?" She came prancing across the floor to him.

"I am standing here—waiting."

Her palm slid under his sac and nimble fingers gently squeezed his balls, putting him on his toes. She rammed her breasts into him and pressed herself hard against him. Then she turned her face up, eyes closed, for his mouth to meet hers.

"Tonight I will make you forget all the women in your life," she said.

Tall order, but he'd sure try her. He nodded for her to continue as their lips met. A hot tongue snaked past his teeth and she was lashing his mouth with it. She began to rub her pubic patch on his upper leg.

Her frantic hand began to pump up an erection. His head swirled, and he spun her around and bent her over with her hands braced on the chair seat. Then he spread her butt and pushed the stiff aching dick against her wet gates. With her hand, she inserted him, and she bowed her back when he pumped it in her.

"*Madre de Dios,* such a wonderful wand." She bent lower so he could enter her deeper. His hands cupped under her and played with her swinging breasts. Surging in and out of her, he became dizzy with the action, and he gripped her hips while pouring the meat into her. Their coupling went on and on until he felt the tingling sensation deep down. His flank went tight against her firm butt and his stick exploded.

She collapsed, and he had to hold her up until she regained her senses. Recovered, she twisted and threw her arms around his neck. Her kiss was sweet and she clung to him. "The water may be cool . . ."

"I don't care," he said, and helped her into the tub.

"I'll get more . . ."

They slid down in the tub. Straddling him, she closed her eyes as if overcome by pleasure and began soaping a cloth. "Judas, you are wonderful."

"Good."

"No, it is not. At sunup, you will leave me." She made a pouty face.

He cupped her left breast. Raising it out of the water, he bent over to kiss it and she rose for him to do it. "We can go till then anyway," he said.

"Ah, *sí.* We can make love all night long, huh?" She dropped the cloth and took his head in her hands to keep him working on the rock-hard nipple he was teasing with his tongue.

Slocum wasn't as certain as she sounded about doing it all night long, but at the moment, she tasted like candy and he had a big sweet tooth to satisfy. They kissed, washed, kissed, and then rinsed, dripping water on the tile floor as they stepped out of the tub. He held her by the arms and kissed her hard.

She dried him furiously fast, and then turned the towel on her luscious creamy brown body beaded in droplets.

Satisfied at last, she tossed the towel aside and charged him. With her firm breasts in his midsection and her pubic bone against his upper leg, she took his breath away by jerking on his hardening erection.

Then they scrambled on the bed. She caught his face and they kissed, with her hot tongue searching his mouth. Still kissing, they twisted until she was underneath him. Her shapely knees raised and spread apart for him. Then she scooted down for his entrance.

When the head of his dick slipped inside her, she sucked in her breath and then gave a cry. He wondered if she wanted the entire house to know what they were doing. But the notion quickly evaporated. His butt wanted to sock it all in her to the hilt, but her contracting ring felt restrictive at each stroke. Moaning, she raised her hips off the bed to meet him, and he surged past the ring.

"Madre de Dios . . ." She closed her eyes behind the thick lashes.

"All night?" He shook his head, never missing a beat. She was beautiful, her breasts firm under his chest. Then her nail-like clit began to score the top of his hard-on each time he went in and out.

Her moans became louder. She tossed her long dark hair in her face and with breathless words urged him onward.

Then she gripped his arms, arched her back, shoved her pubic bone at him, and strained. All at once, she fainted and he felt the rush of fluid around his shaft.

"Oh, m-my—God," she mumbled, and threw her arms back on the bed.

He leaned down to whisper in her ear. "It isn't over yet. Get ready."

He reached under her, cupped the firm cheeks of her ass in his hands, and began to probe her hard. Hip bone to hip bone, he rocked on top of her. The walls began to contract and their breath grew short. Then he gave a deep lunge and from the bottom of his sac came a fountain that filled her.

Raised up on straight arms so his weight was off her, he smiled down at her. "How was that?"

"Wonderful," she managed, and wiggled under him. "But I can't do this all night." She shook her head in disbelief.

"Oh?"

"Get down here and hold me."

He laughed and obeyed her. Morning would be there soon enough. *Damn it, Little Britches, I'm coming for you.*

14

The temperature at predawn was cool in Lucia's yard. Two
pack mules were loaded with bedding, food, and supplies for
him. Maybe enough for an army, Slocum discovered while
checking the panniers and then helping the workers tie them
down with a diamond hitch over the canvas tops.

"I don't know how we can ever repay you," Lucia said,
busy ordering them around and looking like she'd missed
someone or something. "But you know you can come and
rest and relax here any time and stay as long you like."

"Yes, I know that. Thanks, but what is wrong?" he asked.

"The gold bars St. John took. I need them back. I can't
pay my workers without them. I owe money to the Bank of
Sonora in Guaymas."

"If I can recover the bars, I will have them shipped there
or take them there and deposit them in your name."

"Slocum. I owe you my life. How can I repay you?"

"There is no need to worry about that. You and I have
bonds deeper than that."

She nodded and bit her lip. "But Vegas—"

"He is a good man for you."

She looked around and lowered her voice. "Where is
Kalia?"

"Sleeping. She was worn out."

A smug smile behind her lips, she nodded as if pleased by his answer. "She'll be too sore to walk. But I could have told her that. The Yaqui is not here yet."

She spotted someone and shouted to him. "Where is his man, Benito?"

"Coming, Señora. He is on his way."

"Does he have a horse?" she asked.

"No, but I have one for him."

She waved the man on. As if satisfied, she took Slocum by the arm and once they were around the wall, she whirled him around and hugged him in the shadows.

"I am so grateful to you." She looked up and shook her head. "And you wore her out? I am impressed, but I should know. Vegas will be good for me. He is a strong man and will learn the business in time."

"Yes, he will be a good one," Slocum agreed.

"Kiss me. I think your man is out there."

He did, and when he released her, she sighed. "I remember how it felt. Lucky Kalia. I may go wake and tease her. Take care of yourself, find that girl, and kill that *bastardo* St. John for me. And do what you can about my gold."

"I'll try to oblige you. Where is Vegas?"

"He is still sedated or he'd've been here. You must be careful." She hugged him quickly and stepped back.

He could still recall her body naked in the bed with him. Damn, he better go meet his guide. Lucia ran for the house. He stepped back around and met Vic, as they called the small Indian.

"Vic, you have been in the Madres before?" Slocum asked in Spanish.

"*Sí*, and I can speak English, too." The short man grinned.

"Good, we'll talk in English. These kidnappers and killers have taken flight north toward the bronco country."

"They took your woman?"

"Yes. Little Britches. I followed them but had no supplies, and the horse I rode was done in."

Vic nodded as if satisfied. "If they are up there, we will find them."

With the cinch on his saddle tight and his Remington in the boot, Slocum dropped the stirrup, satisfied he was ready, and swung aboard Red. He waved to the gathered workers, and then rode out with Vic leading the mules. He hoped it all went well for them at the mine and that he and Vic would find Little Britches.

Vic impressed him more and more as the day wore on. First, the man never complained. He could still read the two-day-old tracks. Also, he explained to Slocum as they rode about the many places where those outlaws could have gone to hide. The day passed swiftly. They made camp high in the mountains near a small spring that watered the animals. The open highland meadow provided some grass for them to graze.

"Why are you at the mine?" Slocum asked.

"My late wife Lisa." He crossed himself. "Her family all worked at the mine. When I married her I told her I could work there, too. So when she died I stayed there."

"Many of your people are across the border."

"They have to go there. The *federales* chased them from their land on the river."

"You don't wish to join them?"

He wrinkled his nose and squatted down on the toes of his sandals to look at Slocum. "I am more Mexican now than Yaqui." He held up the cross from around his neck. "You know, the padres left us for many long years, and we had our own church without them. So it is different than the other one."

"Catholic is Catholic, isn't it?"

"Oh, *sí*, but we have things they don't have and they have things we don't have." Vic laughed, shrugged, and stirred his beans with a wooden spoon. "So we go to heaven, huh? That is what is important?"

"Yeah, and I ain't in any rush to get there," Slocum said, seated cross-legged on the ground.

"Nor am I."

At daybreak, they had coffee and reheated beans, and were soon on the trail. Slocum had oiled down the Remington with a rag earlier. The long gun looked fine, and he hoped the sight had not been jarred since he last used it.

They moved up to the high ridge and the kidnappers' tracks went over the lip.

"They may go to the Puerta Mine," Vic said, riding along and looking at the prints. "It is all that is over on this side."

"Who runs it?"

"A gringo named Mulkey."

"What's he like?"

"I have no words in English for him. *Malo hombre,* huh?"

Slocum laughed. "Nice guy."

"No, he makes his people work hard for little pay and cheats them at his store. He is no good."

"Why do they work for him?" Slocum asked as they were forced to ride single file on the narrow trail.

"They are afraid he will kill them if they try to leave."

"I guess he'd hide the kidnappers out for a fee, huh?"

"If he could make any money, he would."

Slocum looked off to the lower peaks in the east. Way out there was the Gulf of Mexico. Sandy beaches. Pretty brown-skinned girls to bring you mescal under a grass roof and to do the hat dance for you. He was high in the mountains where the altitude made his head thump and there were no women for miles.

"How far is the mine?" he asked.

"Maybe a day's travel."

"When we get there, can we slip in and see if the kidnappers are there?"

"He has some guards, but they mostly keep the workers in line. No one would come all this way to rob him, the mine is so sorry."

"Why does he keep working it?"

"Oh, they get some gold from it, but if he had to pay help real wages, he couldn't make it."

"I'm concerned about Little Britches." Slocum took off

his hat and wiped the sweat from his forehead on his short sleeve. "She's catching hell from those bastards."

"We'll keep riding tonight."

"Fine with me."

They rode past sundown, and then by the stars. The trail was less perilous, and they finally stopped in a grove of pines a few hours before dawn. Vic wanted to scout at the mine before daylight, and was afraid the mules might give their presence away if they camped too close.

Slocum hitched the stock out of sight and fed them corn in feed bags. After daylight, when Vic did not return, he climbed up higher on a rock formation to survey the entire country. With his field glasses, he could see the mine and the tailing dump. There was little human activity he could make out at the distance. If Vic wasn't back by evening, he'd go look for him. The man might have been forced to hide somewhere down there until dark so he wouldn't be discovered.

Meanwhile, he needed to backtrack up to the last stream they'd crossed in the night and water the horses and mules. In case someone came on the main trail, he kept to the edge of the timber while going there. In two hours, he had them watered and was coming back. He was about to think about a nap when he heard a yip. Only Apaches yipped like that.

Where were they? He dismounted in the cover of the trees and caught the two mules. He didn't need those jack-asses braying at any Apaches. From his place, through the glasses, he saw a handful of the Indians a quarter mile away riding fine stolen horses under good saddles.

What were they doing up there? No telling. No way to warn Vic either that they were coming. They were headed for the mine for some reason. He kept looking at the mules close by—all he needed was for them to start braying.

"Don't move, hombre. Raise your hands slowly."

Slocum froze. He could hear the rowels of the man's spurs approaching from behind. He'd gotten careless. His heart hurt under his breastbone. Captured, he couldn't help anyone. It might even cost him his life.

The man jerked Slocum's .44 out of his holster. "Don't try nothing, hombre. We're going to the mine and see what my *patrón* has for you."

No doubt the swarthy full-faced man, wearing a bandolier that was partially filled with cartridges, meant business.

"What's your name, gringo?" The man motioned him toward the horses with his gun barrel.

"Tom White."

The man laughed. "Well, Señor White, why are you here watching the trail to the mine?"

"I am writing a book. What's your name?"

"Writing a book." The pistolero began to laugh. "Why— why I bet you can't even read."

"I didn't say I was reading one, I said I was writing one."

"Who—who for?" The man was laughing so hard his brown eyes were full of tears.

"For you to read."

"I can't read, stupid."

"And your name is? I want to get it right in the book."

"You are going to put me in the book?" He touched his chest with the muzzle of his handgun.

Slocum shrugged. "If I know your name."

"Pasquel, Pasquel Vansenta."

Slocum nodded as if that made sense to him.

The man looked hard at him. "What would you write about me?"

"I met a pistolero named Pasquel Vansenta in the Sierra Madres."

"Then what you write?"

"He was a man of the gun."

Pasquel nodded. "What else?"

"What is your wife's name?"

He made a face. "I don't want her in that book with me. Get on your horse. Where is the hombre rode here with you?"

"Huh?"

"Two saddle horses. I am not stupid. I followed you to the stream and back here. I never saw him."

"I don't know." Slocum mounted Red. The Remington in

the scabbard under his right leg was empty. He'd be lucky if he ever saw it again. There was always hope, but the sinking feeling in his gut was not cheering him up.

"Ride on," Pasquel said, and gathered mules and Vic's horse to take with them.

"Who are we going to see?"

The man laughed. "Señor Mulkey, the *patrón*."

"Maybe he'd like to be in my book."

"Maybe."

They rode out of the pines toward a log building on an open flat. There were four of the Apache horses standing hipshot in the area in front. The mules began to bray like they could smell Injuns.

Some men rushed out with rifles in their hands and seeing Pasquel, they relaxed.

"Kinda jumpy, ain't they?" Slocum asked.

A big man who Slocum did not know walked out and folded his arms over his chest. This must be Mulkey, the man Vansenta called the *patrón*. Mulkey appeared to be more interested in the mules than in Slocum. "Good mules. We can use them. Kia-enta, get out here."

An Apache appeared in the doorway. He wore a red headband. His nose had been broken several times until it resembled a beak, and the ravages of smallpox scarred his face. With the eyes of an eagle, he looked Slocum over before he even turned to the mules.

"They would do," he said in guttural Spanish. Then, his sinewy arms folded over his sleeveless shirtfront, he considered Slocum. "Who is he?"

"Tom White," Slocum said.

"What the hell you doing up here?" Mulkey asked.

"I'm writing a book." He looked around at Pasquel as if to ask if he could dismount.

The pistolero nodded.

"A book? What about?"

"Mines in the Madres."

"What does he do?" the Apache asked with a frown that furrowed the tight skin on his forehead.

"Writes books."

The Apache shook his head. "How?"

"With a printing press," Slocum said, looking around as if surveying the place for his book.

Mulkey glanced over at Pasquel and shook his head. "Put him in the jail. I don't have time for him now."

"There were two of them," Pasquel said. "There were two saddled horses."

"Then you find the other sumbitch," Mulkey said. "After you lock this one up."

"May I have some paper, pen, and ink to write on while I await you?"

"Huh?"

"If I am going to be in your jail, you should provide me with the instruments to write and paper at least."

"This is my jail." Mulkey used his thumb to thump his chest.

"I know, but even in the most barbaric countries, writers receive those items when incarcerated."

"That's right, you're in a barbaric country all right."

"What harm can pen, ink, and paper do?"

Mulkey shook his head in fury. "Lock him up and find that other dummy that was with him."

"I promise you the International Committee for Jailed Writers will hear about this," Slocum shouted as Pasquel led him away.

"Fuck them, too!" Mulkey shouted after them.

The jail was made of heavy planks and the barred windows were small. Considering the day's rising heat, it would resemble an oven inside by afternoon. Where were the others, St. John, Fine, and the pistolero Angel? He could ask the same thing about Little Britches. He sat down on the wooden bed. That Apache was only there for one reason. Guns. And he'd use Slocum's mules to haul them out, from the sound of things, then no doubt have mule steaks. Apaches would rather eat mule than any other meat.

How would he ever get out of there? Pasquel had no doubt gone back to look for Vic. Another mystery—what had happened to his Yaqui? Slocum mopped his face in his hands. So they thought he was a writer. He might live a day longer. If Mulkey wasn't dealing with the Chiricahua chief at the moment, he'd be asking Slocum pointed questions— really pointed.

Too many questions were unanswered. Damn, this place stank of piss. He rose and began to pace back and forth. His best chance to survive was to get lots of rest. In the event he escaped, he'd get little or none. He stretched out on the bed, put his hat over his face, and closed his eyes.

"Slocum?"

He woke and said, "Yes." Looking around the shadowy room, he wondered where the person was.

"After dark, be ready to go," the voice said in Spanish.

"*Sí*. Who are you?"

"An amigo. I must go."

"Yeah, thanks, amigo." He sat up drenched in his own sweat. That had been a woman—he did not recognize her voice. Maybe if he'd seen her face or breasts, he'd remember her.

At the least, he had an offer of help. No gun, no horse, this far back in the Madres—it would not be a Sunday picnic to ever get back to civilization.

He heard the mules braying, and dragged the bed over to stand on it and look out the small barred window. As he watched two bucks tussle with a mule gone wild, a smile crossed his face. The animal was dragging them all over the place on his lead rope. Then he managed to kick one of them. The Indian folded, holding his belly and sitting on the ground. The mule tore loose from the other buck and left, kicking his heels over his back and cracking farts.

The Indians and Mexicans all stood and watched him depart, cussing the air blue.

One mule had vamoosed. Slocum and Vic had never had a problem with him. From his perch, Slocum had a good view of the yard. No sign of the kidnappers. It bothered him. Had they gone on already?

Where was Little Britches?

They soon led Red over fitted with a packsaddle and began loading him. Crap. Where was his Remington? His saddlebags? No doubt in the log office that Mulkey came out of when Slocum first arrived. He might have to forget that gun. They had crates of rifles on Red, the other mules, and Vic's horse, too. How many guns did that Kia-enta buy? That many rifles should arm most of the broncos left in the Madres.

The Apaches were drinking. Slocum shook his head. He'd not noticed it before, but it was obvious. They were in the jug. Probably why they got into that fit with the mule. Dangerous business, Apaches, gun sales, and whiskey. A little firewater and gunpowder could sure explode.

Things finally calmed around the main building. The Apaches still had not left because the loaded animals still were at the hitch rack. Slocum could see one buck sleeping seated on his butt alongside the building—passed out.

Satisfied that there was nothing that he could do about anything, Slocum stepped down. He needed a good drink of whiskey. He looked in the water pail—dead bugs and flies floated on the surface. Despite his thirst, he was not that bad off yet.

A woman came with her head swathed in a scarf. She carried two burritos in her hand. She looked around to see if anyone was nearby, then stepped to the barred door.

"Here is some food." Then acting as if she feared someone might overhear her, she lowered her voice. "The woman you seek has left here. Victor will come for you—tonight."

Ah, Vic is alive. Slocum nodded and took the food. The burritos felt warm in his hand and despite his lack of appetite, he was pleased they weren't going to let him starve. Better yet, the news that Vic was going to be available to help him heightened his spirits.

"Gracias."

She nodded and swept away.

He was alone, and took a seat on the bunk to eat. Water to drink would have been nice, but he didn't need it.

If Mulkey thought he was just some loco gringo author, that was fine, but Slocum didn't like that Apache. Kia-enta hadn't recognized him as a former army scout—no telling when his memory might recover. Not that Slocum recalled the Apache, but there was no telling where he might have observed him.

Kia-enta might have been part of the bunch that stayed mainly in Mexico, save for the disastrous planned attack they'd made on the small army patrol near the Whetstones, almost in plain view of Tombstone. Perhaps this Kia-enta had taken the place of the leader, who later fell off his horse into a creek and drowned or died of a heart attack. One thing, after this day he'd be better armed with the rifles he'd bought from Mulkey.

Somehow, the worthless Freddie Fine had made this gun deal, but the woman who brought Slocum the food said the kidnappers and the woman had gone on. Why hadn't they stayed there at the mine? They weren't running away from Slocum. No, they could hardly know he was on their trail. Someone or something else had them on the go.

Then he heard the first cannon-propelled grenade explode in the yard outside the jail. He jumped on the bed to see the cause. The Apaches may have been drunk, but the first round sent them scurrying around like wild ants, which spooked the pack mules and horses in the dust cloud.

The Mexican army was coming. The Apaches knew better than to stand and fight a mountain howitzer, and even before the second shell was looped in, Kia-enta and his bucks were northbound *ki-yacking* like coyotes and slapping horse butts with leather in their haste.

Slocum ducked at the whistling scream of the next incoming round. He had only a second to pray the explosive was not going to hit the jail, and was relieved when it fell on the far side of Mulkey's headquarters. From his war experience, Slocum knew the cannoneer had his orders not to hit the structures that might contain gold. He smiled to himself—as long as they thought the jail might contain more precious contents than one gringo, he was safe.

A woman rushed inside and fumbled with a key in the brass lock on the chain.

"Here," Slocum said, seeing that her unfamiliarity and shaking hands were getting nowhere. "Let me try."

He inserted the key and twisted. The hasp fell open, and she nodded and backed up for him to come out. "Victor has horses," she said. And motioned toward the back.

"I can't wait."

Her skirt whirling around her legs, she led the way, checking outside where the dust boiled up from another incoming round that confused the armed men shouting and rushing about. She looked back at him. "Now."

They ran out, and Slocum scooped up a sombrero off the ground. He fastened it on his bare head in his haste so they wouldn't mistake him for a fleeing gringo. They rounded a jacal, and he saw his Yaqui tracker seated on a half-spooked horse, holding out the reins of another bushy-maned mustang.

Slocum grabbed the woman by the arms and kissed her hard on her ungiving lips, causing her brown eyes to fly open in shock. "You're an angel. God bless you."

Then he was on the horse, in the old saddle that was too small for him, with the stirrups too short. But he and Vic were leaving the mine in the same direction the Apaches had gone. He was using the sombrero to make the stiff-legged pony go faster.

"What brought the *federales* up here?" Slocum asked as they rode hard through the head-high scrubby juniper and into the canyon.

"They must have learned about the gun deal."

Slocum looked back and then he nodded. Probably so. Still, too many things were unanswered. Worse yet, where was Little Britches?

15

Slocum sat on his butt and gnawed on some hard jerky. They didn't need to build a fire to cook *pinole*. No telling where in this mountain vastness one or more Apaches lurked. Vic sounded satisfied he'd found the tracks of St. John and company. Kia-enta and the Apaches had split off to the east, and the Yaqui felt satisfied that earlier the kidnappers had gone westerly.

When they'd stopped, Vic had handed him an older cap-and-ball Colt. He thanked the man. Under his examination, he discovered the weapon was loaded and had fresh-looking copper caps on the nipples. The gun had been oiled and cared for over its life. Still, he never considered such an older model as a hundred percent reliable. Later models and cartridge ammunition were a better bet unless he had loaded the weapon himself and knew the powder quality. Still, he felt grateful for the Colt. At least he was armed.

"Any notion where they might be going?" Slocum asked him.

Vic shook his head. "There are some abandoned ranches along the foothills and a town or two. They might go to Agua Sierra."

"What's there?"

Vic shrugged his shoulders. "A mission church, a couple of cantinas, a store, the usual. It is a poor village."

"How far is it?"

"We can be there by sundown."

"We better check it out."

Vic agreed and they mounted up. Slocum had let out the stirrups, but aside from the pony's backbone, riding bareback might have been better than using the old saddle.

They rode up to Agua Sierra after dark. Under the stars, they watered their horses in the rushing stream at the edge of the smattering of jacales, and then went into the square where the trumpet music flowed out of a cantina.

"They know you," Victor said as they hitched their horses at the rack. "So keep your head down. I can do the talking."

Slocum agreed with a bob of his wide-brimmed sombrero and followed Vic inside. The scream of some excited *puta* sounded over the loud music.

One of the women rushed over to appraise Vic as he studied the room's contents. Mostly Indian, she was not pretty, her eyes too squinty in the corners, nose too wide, and lips too thick. The low-cut brown blouse exposed her tube breasts, and she shook her ample hips suggestively at them.

"Ah, you are a big man," she said to Vic.

He ignored her and said to Slocum. "Come on, Pancho. We will have some *cerveza*. What is your name?"

She pressed her body familiarly against him and grinned up as if pleased he had asked. "Teeyah."

"Well, Teeyah, get us three *cervezas* and we will sit in the back." Vic nodded toward the rear.

"Ah, *sí, hombres.* Welcome to my small village. The bartender he expects money for his *cerveza.*" She held out her palm.

Slocum pressed some coins in it.

"Gracias, mucho grandes hombres." And she was off.

They found a vacant table in the darker rear against the wall. Settled in, Slocum watched her return with their beer in large ceramic mugs. Foam spilled over the edges. While several customers had looked them over, they soon drew less interest than the vaquero in his leather pants and vest that stomped with another *puta* to the music.

Vic put his arm on her shoulder and spoke softly in her ear. "Teeyah, we look for some gringos and the one they call St. John."

Her oval brown-eyed gaze shifted from Vic to Slocum. The carefree look in them had vanished. Her brown throat moved from swallowing hard. "What is your business with them?"

"They have a woman. An American that they kidnapped."

She nodded woodenly.

"She is a friend of mine."

"They would cut my throat in minute if they knew I told you anything."

"We won't tell them," Vic promised her. "They are here in the village?"

"*Sí.* They are here. That gringo who sells whiskey to the broncos—"

"Fine, Freddy Fine," Slocum said with a disgusted shake of his head.

Vic nodded. "St. John?"

"*Sí,*" she whispered.

"Angel, the pistolero?"

"*Sí.* That *bastardo,* too."

"Where are they?"

"In a casa on the hill. It isn't hard to find, but be careful, they are bad-hearted men."

Vic raised his mug to Slocum. "To our success."

Slocum agreed with a clunk of his mug. "There is an American woman with them?" he asked Teeyah.

"*Sí.*"

He nodded. All they had to do was storm the casa and get her out safely. There was no need to ask if she was all right—he'd learn that when he rescued her.

"*Gracias,*" he said, and squeezed her hand.

A big man burst in the door with a pistol in his hand and

bandoliers of bullets strapped over his chest. "Where is that gringo?"

Slocum realized they were in the darkest part of the room. He shoved her on the floor and drew his gun as he dropped to his knees. He took aim at the large form and fired. The percussion of the pistol shots doused the lights.

The big man's last shot went into the dirt floor. In their panic to escape the cantina, customers and *putas* wedged the back doorway full of squirming bodies. Others raced over the big man's form to get out the front door at any price.

Acrid gun smoke burned the lining of Slocum's nose. On his feet, he stuck the gun in his waistband and pulled Teeyah up. "You all right?"

"Sí," she mumbled in the darkness.

"Vic?"

"I'm all right."

"Who was that?"

"Angel. St. John's man."

"Let's get out of here. Those shots may have warned them."

They headed for the door. Slocum stopped and rolled the big man over, then undid his gun belt and holster buckle. He jerked it off. Angel moaned.

"I'm dying—help me—"

"Like you'd help us? Go to hell." Slocum swept up Angel's pistol. He'd not need it where he was headed. Then Slocum turned his back on him and started out the dark doorway after the other two. The holster set was too big for his waist, so he slung it over his shoulder. Later, he could make a new hole for the buckle.

They mounted up, and Vic hoisted the woman up behind himself on the horse. They rode out under the stars. Slocum looked back but saw no pursuit. That Angel must have thought he was unstoppable to bust into that cantina like that. They'd been lucky.

"How did he know we were in town?" he asked the woman riding alongside.

"There are men in this village would sell their own mother for a *puta*. Someone ran and told him so."

Slocum nodded.

"There. See the lights." Teeyah pointed to the casa on the hillside. Some candlelight shone in the windows and open doors.

Stopped on the trail, Slocum asked, "Is that St. John's place?"

"No. It belonged to Señor Cruz. But he ran for his life when they came."

"I would, too," Slocum said, and dismounted.

"You know this man St. John well?" Vic asked Slocum.

"I had two run-ins with him when I was in charge of guarding the pack trains for the mine."

"I am surprised he is still alive," Vic said.

"You can't always kill everyone. Caught him off guard and got the drop on him so he had to listen to me. I warned him once not to try to rob the mine trains."

"It did no good?"

"Right, he must have been deaf."

"What can I do to help?" she asked, on the ground busy straightening her skirt.

"Does he have any sentries?" Slocum asked, trying to see in the night.

"I'll go see."

"Whoa." He caught her arm. "We didn't bring you up here to get hurt."

"Oh, they won't hurt me. I may hurt them, but the bad one is dead in the cantina back there. I owe you for that." She put her hands on her hips in defiance.

"First, St. John ain't a saint. Freddie Fine is a white slaver. And also, I don't want to risk Little Britches being hurt any worse than she has already been."

Teeyah agreed.

"Now, we'll all three go up there and then decide how to take them."

"Good enough," she said, and they began to close in on the house, using a draw and some junipers for cover.

With Angel's .45 in his fist, Slocum was glad to have a more dependable weapon, though it didn't save the former owner's life.

They stole close enough to see there was no sentry. Using the pungent-smelling juniper bush for cover, they could hear someone talking in Spanish.

"Who's that?" Slocum whispered to her.

"Sounds like Don Mayorga."

"Who's he?"

She wrinkled her nose at him. "Some rich man who hangs around."

"What's he do?"

"Nothing. He is rich."

Slocum nodded and motioned to Vic that he was ready to move in. They began to advance on the casa, both men armed and Teeyah with her skirt hiked to her knees in case they had to run for it.

". . . ah, Señorita, now that you are mine," the man's voice said.

From the open window, Slocum caught sight of Little Britches naked and bound on a bed. Her hands were tied spread-eagle to the sides. *Mine*—what did he mean? Where were the others?

When Slocum dared look again, the bare-assed bastard was crawling on top of her.

"Hold it right there," he shouted, and pointed his gun through the window.

The man bolted upright on his knees with his erection flopping around. "Who in the fuck are you?"

"Vic, get that sumbitch off that bed."

Vic took off in a run for the door.

"Who—who are you?" Mayorga asked, looking around like a cornered coyote.

Vic jerked him off the bed and pressed him to the wall. Teeyah had come in behind Vic, and was cutting the ties off the sobbing Little Britches.

Slocum looked around in the night—nothing. Where had the others gone? Too late again. "Vic, find out from him where'n the hell they went. I'm coming inside."

In moments, he'd holstered the gun and held Little Britches in his arms. Partially wrapped in a blanket, she hugged him tight. "I knew you'd come. I knew it. I told those bastards you'd get them. Oh, Slocum—"

"When did they leave?"

"After they sold me to him—that one over there—" She motioned to the bare-assed prisoner standing against the wall, whose erection had expired.

"He use you?"

She nodded and held up two fingers.

"When did they leave here?"

"Midday. They left Angel behind to kill you if you came here."

He held her tight and patted her back. "I'm sorry. We didn't know anything."

"I'm just glad you came for me." She leaned back, and her eyelashes were wet with tears. "You are the best sight of my whole life." And she squeezed him.

"They mention that I was coming?"

"St. John kept saying, 'You men, Slocum gets here, I'm killing him.' "

"He knew we were coming?"

"Yes, he expected you."

"There's all kinds of things going on up here. Mulkey sold the bronco Apaches rifles."

"Those were Fine's guns." She shook her head, then rested her cheek on his chest.

"How's he figure into the deal?"

"I think he and St. John had the mine together and split the take. They wanted out of the mountains with the bullion they stole from there, but figured you would be after them. So I guess that's why they kidnapped me. So they'd have bargaining power with you."

"What about the guns?"

"They gave them to Mulkey for fresh horses and went

on. They decided they were far enough ahead of you. They sold me to him this morning." With a grim face, she jabbed her finger at Mayorga.

"And left Angel to deal with me? Where are they headed?"

"The springs at John Slaughter's, I overheard them say. Then San Francisco."

He wrapped the blanket around her. "Teeyah, help her bathe and find her some clothes."

"*Sí.* Come with me."

Slocum rose and walked over to the trembling Mayorga. "What did you pay for her?"

"I-I never—"

Slocum grasped the front of his embroidered white shirt in a wad and jerked him close. "If you don't go to talking and fast, I'm whacking off your pecker."

"Eeee!" Mayorga screamed in a high-pitched voice.

"Then your balls one by one."

"Five hundred pesos. But I never knew—I mean, I never knew she was—"

In disgust, Slocum slammed him against the wall. "I know your kind. Money can buy you anything, but right now it ain't saving you, is it?"

"No, but I could pay you. What do you want? How much? Oh, dear God. How much?" Mayorga held his hands up and cowered in fear.

"Why, for ten cents I'd stick a wagon tongue up your ass. Shut up, I need to think."

"What should we do with him?" Vic asked.

"Tie him up. I don't need him signaling the whole damn town that we're up here. Then go check on the horses that are here. We will need some better ones."

Teeyah was helping Little Britches get dressed in the kitchen when Slocum stormed in there. "Is there any food here for us to eat?"

"I think so," Little Britches said, and forced a smile for him while putting on her pants.

"We can fix some," Teeyah said.

"Good. We need to take off after those two, and I don't think we can leave either one of you here. I better go look and see about extra horses."

"Slocum?"

"Yes." He turned to face Little Britches.

"I owe you my life again."

He shook his head. "I was just here to help."

"No, you didn't need to—"

"I needed to all right. Those two scoundrels need to be behind bars or dead."

She waved him on. "Go check on your horses. Teeyah and I can fix food."

He went outside into the starlight. Vic had led up their horses.

"There is another horse in the corral," Vic said, hitching their mounts to the pole pen.

"That must be Mayorga's."

"We still need another if we take both women."

"I'd hate to leave Teeyah to the likes of Mayorga. He'd take out all his spite on her the minute we leave."

"*Sí,* I agree. I can go back in the village and buy another horse, but I have no money."

"Here." Slocum gave him some money, grateful that Mulkey had been so shocked he'd found a writer that he'd never searched Slocum for valuables.

"How many should I buy?" Vic asked, looking amused at the folding money.

"Horses are cheap, huh?" Slocum climbed over and checked on Mayorga's mount in the starlight. It was a stout gray barb stallion. The saddle was hand-tooled. He'd use it, being the biggest. Serve the bastard right to lose his best horse and saddle for what he did to Little Britches.

"In that village, money is short," said Vic.

"Then get us an extra horse with a packsaddle to haul some bedding and things we can find here."

Vic was on his horse and gone into the night. Slocum, satisfied the gray would suit his purpose, went back to the house. He could smell the wood smoke when he entered the room. Teeyah was making a large flour tortilla in her small hands.

"There are cooked frijoles we are warming up," Little Britches said. "Did you find the paint horse?"

He shook his head.

"I think he was turned loose to graze. He's not a bad ride."

"I'll find him at daylight."

She nodded and busied herself stirring the bean pot. "His pistol and holster are on the table."

In the flickering candlelight, Slocum found Mayorga's gun set. He drew out the late-model Colt .45 and held it up to the light. A well-oiled smooth-looking weapon. Much better than Angel's gun. The holster was fancy-tooled and the gun belt wide with fresh cartridges in the loops. He undid Angel's adjusted belt and strapped on the finer set. It felt much better on his waist. He wrapped up Angel's to put in the saddlebags—he might need it, too.

"Vic is getting horses," he said.

"I am going with you?" Teeyah asked.

"Yes. I figure if you stay here that Mayorga might make you pay for his losses."

She nodded grimly. "I have never been over ten miles away from this village in my life."

Slocum wrinkled his nose. "Time you saw the world."

They laughed with her.

How far away were the others? They had a half-day lead. Standing in the doorway listening to the night sounds of crickets and insects, he considered his options. If St. John and Fine thought they had a big lead, they might squander their time going north. Somehow, he didn't believe that. They'd probably ride their horses into the ground—

"How many pack animals do they have?" He turned to look at Little Britches.

"Four."

"All loaded with bullion?"

She nodded. "They had no camping equipment."

"Were they stout horses?"

"Yes, why?"

"Then they have to find villages to stay at."

She nodded. "They were going to get pack mules and supplies here, but something changed their mind. I never knew why."

"Did they know I was coming?"

"I heard St. John tell Angel to stop the gringo when he got to Agua Sierra. That he could meet them at a place called Cienga Springs." She shook her head. "I don't know where that is."

Slocum nodded. "I have been there."

"Where is it?"

"Across the border, beyond Tombstone."

"St. John promised him lots of gold."

Slocum acknowledged he'd heard her. "Lots of it all right."

They wouldn't have to share any with Angel. He wasn't coming to the next party. St. John still must fear Slocum. Good. Anxious men made mistakes.

16

At dawn, they rode away from the casa headed north. They also left the disgruntled bare-assed Mayorga tied and gagged on the floor. Vic rode in the lead, the two women in the middle, then Slocum. The packhorse on a lead trailed them.

Mayorga's fine saddle felt comfortable between Slocum's knees, and the gray barb was a dream to ride. Little Britches, on the paint, looked less pained, and Teeyah was her usual spirited self.

At midday, they were in the base hills and watered at a stream.

"We can reach La Sierra by dark," Vic said, holding the reins as the women went off to relieve their bladders.

"Is that a good place?"

"Oh, it is like all small villages. It was the last time I was there."

"Maybe St. John used it for a stopover."

Vic agreed. "His tracks go that way."

Slocum nodded and looked back at the towering Madres. It would be hotter from there on. They'd miss the cool mountains before they were through with this business. The desert beyond between them and the border was flatter but unforgiving, a land of thorns and bad water holes that were few and far between.

"When were you over this country last?" Slocum asked.

"A few years ago. I worked at a mine in Tombstone."

"This place you spoke of is how far from the border?"

"Three days, if you are going to the Bernallio Springs."

"I know John Slaughter. I trust him."

Vic nodded.

Slaughter would supply them with fresh horses in exchange for their tired ones and not rob them. By the time they got there, they'd need new ones. There was little forage to find and bad water, and pushing them hard would take a toll on their horseflesh.

"How are you doing?" Slocum asked Little Britches when the two returned.

She nodded under the straw sombrero. "I'm fine. Just to be away from those men is wonderful." She swung playfully on his arm. "And of course to be with you."

"I can't guarantee for how long. There's men that are looking for me. I never know when I'll have to ride on."

She nodded. "I know, but I'm happy for the time we share."

He boosted her into the saddle. "Maybe someday you will be able to settle down and have a life of your own."

"Someday, huh, Teeyah?" Little Britches laughed.

"Someday. Maybe, huh?" Her brown face beaming, she turned her mustang after Vic.

"Vic, watch those two, they are scheming."

"I will, Slocum. I will."

The desert's heat waves distorted the saw-edged purple mountains in the distance. Twice during the afternoon, the barb shied sideways at the dry rattle of a disturbed sidewinder in the greasewood close by. Not seeing the serpent, Slocum rode on after the girls leading the packhorse.

The bloody sundown hung on the horizon to finish cooking his brain before it sank into the distant Gulf of California. A purple twilight spread across the land, and the jacales of La Sierra appeared. Dots of candlelight marked many of the buildings, and dogs began to herald the riders' arrival.

"Everyone be careful." Slocum pulled abreast of the others. "There may be bandits or even St. John here. We'll find a rooming house to stay in if it is safe. Vic, you go in and find out what you can. We'll wait here."

"I can go with him," Teeyah said. "They don't know me."

"One way to know St. John," Slocum said. "He carries a nickel-plated pistol with an ivory-carved handle with a steer head on his grips. His mustache is about white, and he pulls on his right ear a lot."

Teeyah nodded. "He is in this place, Victor and I will find him."

"Be careful."

They rode off. Slocum dismounted heavily, grasping the large saddle horn. His sea legs held him up and he nodded over the saddle at Little Britches in the growing darkness.

"Why couldn't we have met—oh, somewhere else?" she asked.

"Ah, you'd've been married and I'd've had to ride on anyway."

She laughed and then, as if caught up in something, she shook her head in dismay. "How bad of me. I'd forgotten Hyrum. But I know now he'd've never lasted for long if we had taken that ranch. Shame, too; he wanted one. His father had the money." She dropped her chin. "But he'd've never lived very long out here. This is a brutal country."

"You've seen the worst side of it." He'd finished loosening the cinches on their horses and turned to her.

She hugged him, and he clasped both sides of her small butt and drew her against him. "The absolute worst. There's ranch folks all over that won't ever experience the things you've been through."

"Yet it is such a tough man's world. No, my husband-to-be would not have survived. One day, St. John shot a poor Mexican for no more reason than the man did not take off his hat for him."

"He's one of those that spoils the rest of the apples in

the barrel." He rocked her from side to side. "This will be over one day soon."

"Then we can make love and not look over our shoulders?"

"I hope so."

"Will we have a bed together tonight?"

"I hope so."

"So do I."

Seated on the ground, they ate some peppery jerky and washed it down with tepid canteen water. The crescent moon soon began to rise and a coyote yipped at it. At the sound of horses approaching, Slocum rose to brush off his seat.

Vic must be coming back.

"They have left," Vic announced as the two of them drew up their mounts. "They were here at midday and rode on."

"And they hired three pistoleros that were loafing around there and out of work to go with them," Teeyah said, handing him a burrito. Then she gave Little Britches another.

"Were these hired guns tough ones?" Slocum asked.

She shrugged. "I talked to a *puta* about them. She was really glad they were gone. She thought they were mean to her and her sisters after they ran out of money and stayed. Bullies, she said."

"Do we have a room?"

"Yes, and there is grain for the horses."

"Good." He went to get the horses ready to go into town. If he'd been by himself, he'd've ridden on. The two women were tough, but not that tough. But they were on the outlaws' tracks and eventually they'd run them down. Patience might be a good thing. The outlaws would get lax, careless, and then Slocum and his friends would swoop in.

They rode single file into the village. Vic reined up at a jacal and a bent-over woman came out with a candle lantern to meet him. They spoke softly in Spanish, and the rest dismounted. Out of habit, Slocum shifted the Colt on his hip, looking around in the night.

Vic gathered the horses. "The corral is in back. She said they delivered the feed I ordered."

"I'll help you get them settled," Slocum said.

"Give me the packhorse," Teeyah said. "We will unload it."

Slocum agreed, and he and Vic took the other horses.

After watering them, he and Victor curried the horses' backs as the animals crunched corn in the nose bags. Teeyah soon brought the unloaded packhorse. While it was being watered and fed, Slocum left Vic and Teeyah to wait for it to finish.

Little Britches met him and hooked an arm in his. "I have the hammock ready."

"Good. They may be coming shortly."

"No," she said softly. "Teeyah has plans so we can be alone."

"Oh. Fine," he said.

In minutes, they were undressed and on the bouncy hammock. He was between her raised knees and bent over to taste her rock-hard nipples. She pulled his face up to hers and they kissed long and hard. His hips began to beg to probe her, and his rising erection ached to enter her gates.

Her small fingers closed on his shaft and guided it homeward. With her thin legs wide apart, he drove it home and she gasped, clutching him until her fingernails dug into his arms. He could feel her hard nail-like clit scratching the top of his shaft as they plunged in and out of passion's arms.

His erection reached its fullest proportions and the head felt ready to split open as they continued, aided by the rocking of the hammock. At last, fire rose from his aching testicles and his molten lava spewed into her. They collapsed in each other's arms and fell asleep.

At dawn, Teeyah returned with breakfast in a tortilla for each of them from a street vendor. The horses, watered and saddled, were ready to go. Slocum paid the old woman for the night and they rode on, eating their food on the trail.

At mid-morning, Slocum saw the dust boiling up in the north. When he pointed it out to Vic, the Yaqui nodded as if he'd already seen it.

"Who is it?" Little Britches asked him, motioning toward the dust.

"Could be the army."

"Whose?"

"Federales."

She nodded.

When he could see the flapping guidon, Slocum realized they were Americans, and when they drew closer, he could see the Apache scouts. He stopped his companions and waited.

An officer, a scout, and a noncom rode up.

"Good day, sir," the officer said to Slocum, and he took off his hat for the women.

"Good day, Lieutenant. What can we do for you?"

"Are you Slocum?"

"Yes." Slocum frowned.

"Sergeant, arrest this man and his associates."

"What in the hell for?"

"I have two sworn witnesses that you and your associates sold arms to the bronco Apaches."

"What witnesses?"

"There will be due time in court to inform you of all this information. You are under arrest for selling firearms to the combatants."

"I want you to know I rode with General Crook. He will vouch for me."

"Then you have no worries. Are you surrendering your firearms?"

"This is a mistake that you'll regret, Lieutenant."

"Not likely, sir. Not likely."

"Did those men who swore to you that I sold guns to the broncos use the name Fine and St. John?"

"Slocum, it will all be available at your hearing."

"Those men have thousands of dollars of gold on those

packhorses that they stole from a mine in the Sierras. That's why we're trailing them."

"Your handgun, sir."

Slocum lifted it slowly and handed it over. "I'll be at your court-martial."

Damn—what next?

17

"Lieutenant Kennedy! You arrested the wrong men!" Captain Dansin shouted.

Slocum shook his head in disbelief as he sat the weary gray and looked at the red-faced veteran officer. For the past three days, he'd repeatedly told the shavetail who arrested him and Vic for gunrunning that he had the wrong men and the real villains were escaping.

"This man has served the army well. Who told you he was a gunrunner?" the superior officer demanded.

"I have the sworn statement of one Henry St. John and a Frederick Fine that this man Slocum sold arms to the Apaches in Mexico."

"Fine is a well-known border gunrunner himself, and who is this St. John?"

"A damn Mexican bandit," Slocum said, and dismounted in disgust. "I've been telling him that for three days, and in the meanwhile, they have gotten away with enough gold to buy a ship."

Dansin shook his head. "I'm sorry. And good day, ladies, welcome to Camp Harold. I am sure it is at least shadier in my tent."

"We accept your invitation," Little Britches said, and

nodded firmly to Teeyah. They both dismounted, and a private caught their reins.

Slocum looked over the row of wall tents set up across the border on the Arizona side. He turned to the gray and undid his girth.

"Where did they go?" Dansin asked. The captain showed his age, his mustache frosted and the girth of his waist expanded from his lean days of chasing bronco Apaches in Mexico.

"I understood they were planning on crossing at the Slaughter Ranch," said Slocum. "No doubt to miss any customs inspection. But they probably did that two days ago by my count."

"Would they go to Tombstone?"

"I have no idea. They could cross over Muleshoe Pass and get there in a day."

"I can send a man up to the telegraph line and wire Marshal White. He'd arrest and hold them if they're there. Sheriff Behan, I don't trust."

"It's worth a try. I'd appreciate it."

"Sergeant Mayes, get a messenger saddled and ready to ride."

"Yes, sir. Corporal Ross, go find Private Yates and have him mounted when he reports."

"I'll get him, Sarge."

Dansin nodded and showed Slocum and Vic to his tent. "I can't believe that lieutenant arrested you."

"Hey, he's young and eager."

"That's no excuse. What can I do to help you?"

"We'll wait for a reply to your wire and then decide which way we must go."

"Wait." Dansin looked reflectively at the tent ceiling. "The army has a squad of men stationed at Slaughter's ranch. They're out of Fort Bowie. I'll send word to them. Perhaps they know something about the two men's passage." He turned to his orderly with instructions to write a telegram to Marshal White regarding the two and to send a man to the Slaughter Ranch to learn from the men stationed there what they knew about St. John's and Fine's destination.

"Ladies." Dansin swept off his hat. "Sorry I was so busy, but I have not had the pleasure of meeting you."

"That's Silver Temple, better know as Little Britches," said Slocum. "And that is Teeyah."

"I hope the army hasn't mistreated you. I am sorry for the inconvenience. I see they brought you refreshment."

"We're fine," Little Britches said for both of them.

"What can I do for all of you?"

"Some cots and a place to sleep," Slocum said. "We can use some catch-up sleep while we wait for word."

"Sergeant Mayes can handle that."

"Wonderful," Little Britches said, and smiled.

By sundown, the telegraph messenger was back. Marshal White's reply stated he had not seen nor heard of the two men being in the area. He would watch for them. Then the soldier from Slaughter's ranch rode in.

"Sergeant Kelly reports that the party in question, sir, was headed for Silver City."

"Anything else, trooper?"

"No, sir."

The young man saluted and hurried off. When the captain turned back to Slocum, they shared a nod.

"Now you know that much."

"Thanks. We'll leave for there in the morning," Slocum said. They had a trail to follow. Maybe it would lead them to the pair and the gold.

Back at the tent, the other three were busy eating. Little Britches looked up and smiled. "Your food is here."

She motioned to a plate heaped with browned sliced beef and potatoes. "Real food."

"She means no tortillas," Vic teased.

"Well, they supposedly went to Silver City, New Mexico," Slocum said.

"How far away is it?" Little Britches asked.

"Several days' ride. We leave in the morning. If any of you wish to return to your homes, I don't have much money to pay you, but I can write a letter to Señora Valenta and she will pay you for your time and troubles."

Teeyah and Vic shared a questioning look at each other. "What do you wish to do?" she asked him.

"Maybe go back to the mine," Vic said, and put his arm on Teeyah's shoulder. "We talked about what we'd try when this was over," he said to Slocum.

Teeyah grinned. "If he can stand me for that long."

"I'm sure he can," Slocum said. "I wish you both good luck and good fortune."

Vic looked concerned. "But that will mean there is only you and her against those two, or maybe more."

"We'll be careful."

The Yaqui nodded.

Dansin had a stray horse and packsaddle in his stable that he gave them. The goods were split up, and Slocum shook Vic's hand. "Be sure to take that letter I wrote to Lucia," Slocum said.

"Ah, *sí, amigo.* I enjoyed working for you very much."

Slocum gave him ten pesos and shook his head. "Ride carefully."

Vic agreed and mounted up. About to cry, Teeyah waved, and they rode off.

"Well, we've thanked the captain, let's get out of here." Slocum threw his leg over the gray and he and little Britches left the camp.

Four days later they arrived in Denning, a dusty railroad town on the high flats along the Southern Pacific rails. It was the terminal end of the SP's westward expansion due to national financial circumstances. Slocum and Little Britches stabled their horses at Ace High Livery. Then Slocum showed her inside the Palace Hotel.

"Ah, Mr. and Mrs. Tom White, how nice to have you as our guests," the clerk said after Slocum signed them in. The man was looking hard at her clothing.

"We'll need a bath in our room," Slocum said to the stiff-necked clerk.

"That'll be twenty-five cents more."

"Fine." Slocum paid him, took the key, then held his elbow out for her. "My dear. The water will be up shortly."

"Oh, yes, oh, yes," the desk clerk said.

Upstairs in the room, she laughed. "My, he didn't approve of my clothes, did he?"

"I may need to find you a dress."

She wrinkled her nose. "I'm content. Though these could use being washed."

"They can have that done. I need to go check on some things and get a bath later."

"Fine." She turned her face up for him to kiss her, and then gave him a hug. "Be careful."

"I'm always that."

At the desk, he ordered a robe sent up to her and gave instructions to have her clothing washed. On the boardwalk, a dust devil caught him in its funnel of wind, dirt, and paper trash. Forced to grab for his hat to save it, he blinked his gritty eyes and grinned after it. The spiral spun away, danced down the street, and caused two spooked horses to break loose from the hitch rack.

They shied into a wagon, and the cussing teamster struck the near one with his whip. That caused the cow pony to tuck tail and run. The second one ran after in pursuit, leaving two red-faced cowboys shouting more obscenities at the driver.

Slocum parted the batwing doors and stepped in to the first saloon. It was dark and smoky inside. He sidled over to the bar and ordered a shot of rye.

"Two bits," the barman said, and poured him one.

Slocum paid him, and added another half-dollar. "That's for information. I'm looking for two men passed through here a few days ago."

"And what was their handle?"

"Freddie Fine and Henry St. John."

The man looked in deep reflection, arms folded. He squeezed his chin. "Two days ago."

"Say where they were going?"

"No, but I bet Norma could tell you."

"Who's she?'

"A whore. I'll send someone up and get her if you're willing to pay her."

"Yes, I'll pay her. I'll be at the back table. Give me that bottle and an extra glass."

"Four bucks."

He paid the man, who'd already pocketed the half-dollar.

"She'll be here shortly."

Slocum downed his own drink, nodded to the man, then took the two glasses and his bottle to the back table. Several railroad men sat at a round table smoking cigars and playing poker.

"Got a seat," one of them offered.

"Maybe later."

"Do that. We could sure use some new blood in this game." The others laughed.

In a short while, a tall woman of ample proportions in a blue lacy dress appeared. She spoke to the barkeep and he pointed at Slocum. She came slinking over, shaking as much as possible and causing the poker men to take the cigars out of their mouths to admire her. She grinned at their whistles, and blinked her heavy lashes at Slocum, who'd stood up and removed his hat for her.

"Sweet Jesus, a gentleman." She swept the dress under her and took the seat he pulled out for her.

"What kin I do for you?"

"Tom White. Norma, the barman said you knew all about Freddie Fine and Henry St. John."

"They both got small dicks." With a laugh, she reached over and poured whiskey into her glass. Raised it in a salute to him and took a sip. "They must owe you money."

"They owe me all right. Where were they headed from here?"

She crossed her legs, exposing enough shin for a look-see, and pointed the glass at him. "What's it worth to you?"

"Two dollars."

She stopped and acted as if she was considering it. "You've got a deal." Then she downed some more whiskey.

He put the money on the table.

"They were going to Keersum."

"Where's that?"

"About thirty miles north and to the west." She made a face and, ready to take another drink, she held the glass close to her lips. "It ain't no church picnic grounds. A bunch of hard dicks hang out up there."

"Sounds serious."

She finished taking her drink and drew the back of her long hand over her mouth. "I was there once and I ain't going back. I was so damn sore I couldn't walk, and on top of that they stole the money I made. Bastards."

"How can I get in there?"

She shook her head. "That is a tough bunch. They don't trust anyone either. Cotter Bates runs it like a king. Hell, the sheriff don't even go up there."

"Why did those two go there?"

"Running from the law, I guess. Freddie Fine's been there before. They supplied him with rifles they stole about three months ago."

"So I guess he went up there to pay his bill."

"Probably—that damn Cotter Bates's got a cock bigger than a stud horse." She made a whistle and reached for the bottle.

He poured her some more. "How would they sell lots of bullion?"

"Make a deal with some mine at Silver City."

"Could they do that up there?"

"They could do anything they wanted up there." She laughed and put her hand familiarly on his leg, then looked him in the eye. "You're a nice guy. I'd give you a helluva toss in my bed if you needed one for that money you paid me."

"I'm fine. Can you think of anything else about those two?"

"I figured they'd made a haul. They were showing off lots

of money. Must have cashed some gold. That Freddie Fine's got a rep as a white slaver, so I watched him. The Mex was a tough one, figured he'd cut your throat if you crossed with him."

"Where would they cash gold?"

"Any bank."

"You don't know which one?"

She shook her head. "They had paper money in all their pockets."

A snicker snuck out, and then she laughed. "You know all that money won't grow them a bigger pecker. They needed one apiece."

"That's good enough. Take the bottle."

She blinked in disbelief at his offer. "I've got lots of time. What is it, four o'clock?"

"Trouble is I don't. Keersum?"

"Yes." Her smooth forehead wrinkled in a frown and her blue eyes were seriously set. "Better cover your asshole. That's a bad place."

"To another time and place." Slocum slapped his palms on the table to push off.

"I'd bet one thing."

"What's that?"

"You sure don't need a bigger dick and them bastards better cover theirs." Her laughter rang out. She jumped up and kissed him. "I love you, big man. Don't forget my name's Norma."

He left the bar, walked to the barbershop, and stepped inside. The man was in the chair reading a newspaper.

"Am I too late for a shave, haircut, and bath?"

The man checked his pocket watch. "Lord, no, I'm open till eight at night."

"Kinda late hours, ain't they?"

"Aw, them railroaders come in late in the day and I need the business."

Slocum nodded and sat in the chair. He undid the kerchief around his neck, and the man covered him with a sheet.

"Cattle buyer or drover."

"Uh-huh."

"Figured you was one when I looked up and saw ya. I don't miss many. Guess cattle prices are still good. The town butcher was in last week. Said he paid two bits a pound for some fat cattle. The drover said he had them sold to an army contractor in Arizona for that much."

"Paid a dime or eight cents a pound for them in Texas. That ain't a bad profit."

The barber whistled over the figure as his scissors clacked away and clips of hair rained down on the sheet.

"A fellow was in here a few days ago. Said them Apaches was on the warpath again down in Mexico."

"I hadn't heard."

"Yeah, his name was Fine. Businessman that's been down there. Said them Apaches might be back up here—soon."

Fine should know—he sold them the guns. That worthless bastard.

18

Little Britches jumped up from her seat on the edge of the bed when he came in the room. Wrapped in a snow-white robe, she ran over and hugged him.

"I'm so glad that you're back."

He kissed her, and then led her over to the window to check the street below. Minutes before, he'd spotted Mulkey and his pistolero riding in on jaded horses. Was his Remington rifle on that horse Mulkey rode? If it was, he wanted it back.

"What is it?" she asked.

"A man might have delivered me my rifle."

"The one with the telescope?"

"That's it."

"Who?"

"Mulkey from the mine."

She shuddered under his arm.

"He used you, too?" Slocum asked.

"Yes. Fine tried to sell me to him."

"He didn't want you?"

"I never moved a muscle the whole time he was—on top of me."

"Oh." He hugged her shoulder. "I guess you had hell with all of them."

"Exactly." She let the robe come open and pressed her bare skin to him. "Hold me and love me."

"After that, we can try to find his horse. I'd like to have my gun back."

"Oh, Slocum." She wet her lips and pleaded. "Make me forget them."

"I'll try, darling. I'll try."

One hour later, they ate supper in a restaurant with white linen tablecloths. Sitting in the booth in the rear suited Slocum fine. He realized the waiter had only considered seating them after Slocum tipped him. In a back booth, a man with a mistress could stay concealed.

They sipped a red wine and ordered their waiter's recommendation—young lamb chops with mint sauce. When the waiter left them, Little Britches smiled. "Hyrum would have liked this place."

"You miss him?"

"No. I just thought about him."

"Why was that?"

"It's a terrible thing for me to even say." She lowered her voice. "But Hyrum had a thing as small as those other two—St. John and Fine."

Slocum reached over and squeezed her forearm. "You're getting better if you can laugh at it."

"Maybe. It's always better when I am with you."

"We get finished here, we need to go find my gun."

"Yes. We may need it."

"Exactly."

When supper was over, he paid the bill and they slipped out the back way. In the dark alley, they scattered stray cats and walked around trash heaps to the livery. At the back doorway, he checked to see if there was a swamper about. He didn't see one, and they eased inside to check through the saddles.

None of the saddles straddling the wall had his gun in the scabbard. They walked a block, and after being sure they were not observed, slipped in to the Lone Star Wagon Yard. A few minutes later, she hissed to him, "Over here."

It was his rifle all right. He eased it and the forked stick out of the scabbard, while she dug the cartridges out of the saddlebags. With a nod, they started for the back of the livery. Moments later, a half block away, they both breathed easier.

"Whew. You have your rifle back." She rested her butt against he building and shook her head in the starlight. "I was about shaking back there, I was so afraid."

"We're safe now." And he did have the long-range rifle in his hands again.

They were entering the hotel from the back entrance. A loud familiar voice in the lobby made him stop her.

"Mulkey," he said to her. "He's in the lobby."

She listened, then nodded in agreement that it was him haggling with the clerk.

". . . I want that writer sumbitch. What room's he in?"

"I can't give you that information. I am certain that when Mr. White returns this evening, he will be glad to discuss anything you like."

"I'm going to kill the sumbitch, too."

"I hope not in this hotel."

"Hope your ass. I get him in my gun sights, he's dead."

Slocum stood the rifle on its butt and gave it to her to hold. "Stay here."

"Oh—"

Slocum drew out the Colt and checked the cylinder, then jammed the weapon in the holster. Mulkey wanted him, he'd damn sure find him.

He allowed himself a moment for his eyes to get adjusted to the brighter lights, then shoved his hat back and stepped into the lobby. "You looking for me?"

"Why, you lying sumbitch—" Red-faced, Mulkey twisted around to draw his handgun.

The .45 slug from Slocum's muzzle struck Mulkey squarely in the chest and staggered the big man so his revolver went off in to the floor. The percussion of the shots doused the lights. The darkened room boiled with acrid gun smoke. Slocum heard him crumple to the floor.

"Slocum!" Little Britches shouted, and rushed into the room.

He caught her with his left arm. "There was no talking to him."

His six-gun holstered, he herded her out the front door. Along with the desk clerk, who was already on the porch, they coughed and gasped for fresh air.

A lawman ran up and frowned at them. "What was the shooting about?"

"The man in there—" The clerk caught his breath. "He tried to shoot Mr. White."

"Who was he?"

"Mulkey," Slocum said. "A mine operator and gunrunner from Mexico."

"Don't sound like the world will miss him." The law turned back to the clerk. "Self-defense, you say?"

"Oh, yes, sir. That guy was a raging madman."

"Guess you're passing through, Mister—ah, White?"

"I am, sir."

"Sorry, ma'am, we try to run a peaceful town here."

"I understand," she said, and thanked him.

They went back inside and Slocum left the marshal the chore of disposing of the body. In the back hall, Slocum and Little Britches recovered his rifle, and he took it up to their room to check it out.

"Is it all right?" she asked, leaning on him as he examined it.

"I think so. No one ever shot it. Looks clean enough."

"Where to next?"

"A place called Keersum. Those two might be hidden there."

"What if they aren't?"

"I guess go to Silver City and check on them there."

"Get undressed," she said, then stripped the suspenders off her shoulders and began unbuttoning her shirt.

"What for?"

"What for?" Her eyes flew open. With a scowl, she gave

him a two-handed shove. "Because I sure aim to use you and this bed for all it's worth tonight."

"My, my, where did that sweet girl I found in the desert go?" He toed off his boot and shook his head in mock dismay.

"I have been plowed by more sorry men than I want to count, and you've got a lot of making up to do for all that."

"How could I have helped it?" He paused to look at her compact derriere as she wiggled off the pants. Lots of woman in that small package.

"By what you're going to do tonight."

"Good, I can do that."

Naked as Eve, she blew out the lamp, turned back the covers, and bounced on the bed. "We'll see about that, too."

Dawn came as a blue promise. They had their horses and packhorse saddled and ready to ride. Slocum still fought the cobwebs in his brain. Too much scampering in the bed with her all night and not enough sleep. He slid the rifle in the used scabbard that the swamper sold him for a dollar.

"Keep your hands away from your gun," a rough voice ordered. "I come to talk to you."

Slocum heard Little Britches sharply suck her breath in. He turned around to look at the Mexican sombrero topping the man in the doorway with the six-gun in his hand.

"Ah, Pasquel Vansenta," Slocum said. "You're out of work this morning, I understand."

"You shot my *patrón*."

"No, I shot a worthless bastard that raped her and sold guns to the broncos."

"I have no money. I only wish to return to my homeland."

"Then put that gun away. No need for you to be in a New Mexico prison."

Pasquel laughed. "Why would you give me money?"

"Because you never stole mine."

"Do you have much money on you?"

"Some. I'll give you twenty pesos and you can go home."

Pasquel shook his head and holstered his gun. "I never met a man wrote books before. You are a crazy hombre. First you shoot a tough man, then you give another *dinero*."

Slocum slapped the money in Pasquel's palm. "Ride easy, amigo. There is more work for a good man in Mexico. Maybe working for a better man."

"*Gracias*." Pasquel looked at the paper money he shuffled in his fingers as if considering it. "Say, have you got one of your books?"

"What good would it do you?"

"I can read some."

"It's in English."

Pasquel shook his head. "I don't need a book like that. *Adios*."

Watching him leave, Slocum reached out and hugged Little Britches. They were chuckling to themselves until they heard Pasquel ride off.

At last free of him, she pointed a finger at Slocum. "He wanted a book *you* wrote to read?" And then she broke into tears and laughter.

"I told him he couldn't read it anyway . . ." Too much. He doubled over.

19

They sat side by side at the small campfire. Red-orange tongues licked at the night's darkness. They had eaten some *pinole*—a mixture of ground corn and raw sugar that vaqueros existed on. The cowboys simply added water and cooked it in cups.

"This place we're going is in a canyon?" Little Britches asked.

"Yes. I don't know if they're there or not, but I was warned that a tough hombre runs the place."

"Do we need help?"

"Not much around here."

"You aren't going down there alone, are you?"

"I need to learn if they're there or not."

"I don't like it. It sounds too dangerous. St. John and Fine would kill you in a minute."

"Others have tried."

"Slocum. Listen to me. They will kill you."

"I'll ease down there tonight and check around."

"You're so stubborn—"

He reached over, hugged and kissed her. When their mouths separated, he cradled her in his arms and rocked her. "I'll be fine. You can watch the horses while I'll go down and look."

"I'm scared." She hugged her arms. "This is too danger-ous. You alone."

"I'll put out the fire. There's a place I can get down a side canyon." He poured some canteen water on the blaze, then scuffed dirt on the edges.

She brought the horses up and gave him the reins to his. "I wish we weren't—"

His kiss silenced her, and then he tossed her on the horse with a laugh. "Come sunup, you'll be smiling again."

"That a promise or a threat?"

"Why, a promise of course."

The stars lighted the small mountains in a pearl glaze. He led the way up the steep trail with mesquite brushing his legs as they wound their way skyward. At last, on a great flat that sloped away from them, he told her the hide-out was off the lip to the south.

Dismounted, he hobbled the horses so they could graze the dry bunchgrass. When he finished, he gave her the older-model Colt from his saddlebags.

"It's loaded. You know how to shoot one." He recalled her marksmanship.

She nodded.

"Don't close your eyes when you shoot it."

With a grim look on her face, she agreed.

"I'll be back," he said.

He left her on the rim and eased his way off the steepest part. Far below, he could see a few lights of jacales. The rough rocks soon hurt his hands as he let himself down the sheer wall. At last, he dropped on a ledge and caught his breath. The way down the side canyon became easier, and the brush was tall enough to conceal him. Down to the last hundred yards, the steep ground was covered in low sage-brush. He kept low and hoped no one was watching.

Fifty feet from the first outlying jacal, he dropped to the ground and listened. There was music somewhere. He rose up and dared to pass the dark silent house. Horses were fighting. In the corral, a troublemaker was angry and biting all the sleeping horses, which caused enough confusion.

Dust boiled up and several cur dogs rushed in to add to the melee.

A short Mexican waving a sombrero climbed over the corral fence and tried to separate them. Flying hooves soon flattened him. With dogs biting their heels, the herd stampeded around the pen—not one or two, but perhaps two dozen. Two more Mexicans came into the pen shouting, cursing, and waving sombreros at the panic-stricken horses. The horses crashed into the corral fencing. Poles cracked and the horses escaped in a flood through the opening.

"Get some horses and go after them!" someone ordered in Spanish.

Slocum wanted to cuss. Everyone was awake in the boiling dust that hung in the air. Women rushed about. Men raced around shouting, trying to find horses that had not escaped. A few took reatas and raced off in the direction the horses had fled.

There was no sign of St. John or Fine. Maybe they'd gone on. This Cotter Bates must not have known the value of their bullion, or he'd probably have taken it from them. Busy speculating on his next move, Slocum heard voices speaking in English.

"Now what in the fuck do we do?" It was St. John.

"They'll get them horses back in few hours." Freddie Fine was here, too.

Next problem: Where was the bullion and how could he get it away from them? Crouched behind a smelly outhouse, Slocum tried to see where those two were standing. Damn, he'd never get the drop on them, load the loot, and take it plus them out of there. Bates must have a dozen men on his payroll.

Squatted down in the stinking shadows, he only had a few hours of darkness left, and no telling how long their horse roundup would take. It was no time for him to head back to Little Britches over the lower slopes with no cover. With everyone awake, he'd be an easy target.

"Don't move, Señor."

He spun on his toes and saw the hatless Mexican pointing

a large cap-and-ball Colt at him. His heart stopped. No backup. Damn. All he had left to hope for was that at dawn, if he didn't come back, she'd ride on. *Dear God, please guide her . . .*

In the office of Cotter Bates, brightly lit by lamps, the narrow-eyed half-Chinese sat on the dusty desktop. "What are you doing here?"

Seated in a chair, Slocum stonewalled them for the fifth time, and knew the red-faced man called Dago would hit him again in the face with his fist. The blow made him see stars.

"That loosen your tongue?" Bates demanded.

When he didn't answer, Bates slid off the desk. "Put him in the shed. A few days on no water and food will make him want to tell us everything."

Dago agreed. "Stupid gringo, what did he want anyway?"

"Who knows?" Bates yawned. "I need some sleep."

Dago marched Slocum out of the office into the dawn. A glow had begun in the east. The bare ground that went downhill was steep. The cocky rooster strolling behind Slocum was bragging under his breath how he'd—

When the man gurgled, Slocum turned and heard the thunder of a rifle's report from a faraway gun. Dago was knocked on his butt—hard hit. High on the bluff, Slocum could see the puff of gun smoke. He scooped up the man's pistol, thumbed it back, whirled, and shot the first man that burst out of the office door. That one crumpled, and another sprawled over him.

A rider was coming back hard. Slocum whirled and the man in the saddle froze, then he fell off. The horse spooked away and left bucking as the thunderlike report echoed overhead. It was Little Britches. She'd taken out another Mexican. Slocum reached the security of some packing crates—his four shots would be precious.

The pistol-swinging Bates ran out on the porch in his nightshirt. "What the fuck is happening?"

Another white-clothed Mexican charged down the slope waving his pistol. Slocum stopped him with round two.

Three shots left in the old cap-and-ball. Bates came—his gun smoking bullets that smashed into the building behind Slocum. Steadying the heavy pistol with both hands, Slocum aimed and fired it. The bullet took the raging Bates in the face and he fell over backward.

The Mexicans began to run in all directions. One more, instead of trying to escape, came screaming like a banshee from the office. He had his pistol in hand, his poncho waving behind him—a heavy slug from the mountain struck his chest and punched him backward.

Too weary to get up, Slocum slumped on the ground. He needed to wave the all-clear at her, if she could recognize him in the telescope sight.

Where were St. John and Fine? On his feet, he started across the open ground littered with bodies and waved his hat. He couldn't see her at the distance. He only hoped she knew it was him.

When she didn't shoot him, he felt better and slogged on toward the office. Where were those other two? He climbed the steps and stepped over the dead man on the porch. There on the office floor was something covered by dirty canvas tarps. With his left hand, he swept the covering back in a flurry of dust and saw the panniers. Were they the ones he'd come after? Could he be so lucky?

He stuck the six-gun in his holster and knelt down to unbuckle straps on the first one. In the pannier, he found several sacks of high-grade ore, gleaming in gold flakes. For a second, he wondered why they'd only taken rich ore. Then he ran his hand down in the rich material and struck something solid. It was heavy and required both hands to lift.

A gold ingot—they could bring unrefined ore across the border without paying a tariff. With bullion, they'd pay a heavy fee. He sat on his butt and then brushed his hands off over the open pannier. The reflective gold dust clung to his hands and forearms. *I have your gold, Lucia.*

The sounds of horses coming awoke him from his half daze. Where was he? Seated on his butt beside the treasure he'd come for.

"Slocum! Slocum!"

"I'm coming, Little Britches." He struggled to his feet and made it to the doorway. At first sight, she bounded off her horse and raced up on the porch.

"You all right?" she asked.

"Fine. How are you?"

"I may never use my arm again. That damn gun kicks like a mule." She shook her head.

He hugged her gently, observing her stiff right arm and the shoulder that must be sore. "You see Fine and St. John ride off?"

"Yes. I thought they were too far away to shoot at. Besides, they were going behind things."

"No problem. They're gone. We have the gold."

"What next?"

"Get the gold bullion to Wells Fargo in Denning and have them deliver it to Lucia's bank."

"Then what?"

"Hell, I don't know. Go back to Dragoon Springs—I never asked you what you were going to do."

She buried her face in his shirt. "I ain't through with you yet."

"Good—for now."

"What should we do now?"

"I'll round up some packhorses, and the sooner I get this to Wells Fargo the better."

"I'll go, too. This place is spooky."

"Good," he said, and ushered her out the front door. On the barb gray, he swung around. "I'd like to get my strawberry roan back, too."

"He with them?"

"No, the damn Apaches took him for a packhorse. Probably ate him by now."

They short-loped to the east, and they soon began to see the scattered, loose horses grazing. He swung around them and sent half a dozen back toward the corral and headquarters. They filed obediently into the corral and he dismounted. "You block that break with your mount."

Slocum took down a reata looped over a post and roped the first one. He was well broke and stopped when the loop encircled his head. When he was tied up, Slocum caught a second one and had him hitched. Then, with another lariat off the fence, he picked out a taller horse that bucked around some before Slocum brought him under control.

"He looks tough," she said.

"Aw, he's salty is all. Bet once we get him saddled, he doesn't do a thing."

In thirty minutes, they had packsaddles on the three and the panniers loaded on them. "We only need three?" she asked.

"That should do it." He hugged her good shoulder. "Let's go to Denning."

"Where did all his men go?"

"They ran off when you went to shooting at them and must have run a ways. I haven't seen a sign of them."

"Think they'll track us?"

"Not if I shoot a few of them if they try."

"I'll be glad when we get this gold to whoever and we can get off by ourselves."

He boosted her on the horse and smiled. "Me, too."

They rode all night to reach Denning. His eyes gritty and dry, he focused on the jacales north of the Southern Pacific rails. They crossed the double tracks at first light, weary and tired. He dismounted and entered the terminal depot with the sign WELLS FARGO FREIGHT AGENCY in black letters on the side.

"Wells Fargo man here?" he asked the telegraph operator under the celluloid visor who was clacking on the key.

The man wrote a message on a pad and then shook his head. "Rensaleer is his name."

"Can you get him word? I have a gold shipment for him."

"Bud! Get up here!"

A sleepy boy of ten or so appeared. "Yes, sir?"

"Go up to Milly's Cat House and tell them to get Rensaleer down here. He has business to attend to."

"Yes, sir."

"Don't you dillydally around up there either. Your mother will bust both our asses."

"Yes, sir, Mr. Heinz." With a big grin plastered on his freckled face, Bud left in a run for his destiny.

"You can bring it inside," the operator said.

Slocum nodded. Each pannier contained four canvas bags of ingots and gold ore that weighted fifty to sixty pounds apiece. So he brought them in one at a time and put them on the counter. Little Britches had taken off the hitches and canvas covers.

The operator raised his eyebrows as the pile grew. "You mine all this?"

"No, bandits stole all this in Mexico and I got it back."

Heinz whistled. "Damned if I think I'd've brought it back. Must be paying you good."

"Well, you aren't me."

"That's for damn sure. I hope Rensaleer gets here soon. I'm getting nervous having all this out in the open."

"He should be coming, shouldn't he?"

"Yeah, Bud'll bring him. His mother will probably wallop me if she hears about me sending him up there."

Slocum stopped in the doorway on his way back for another sack. "Guess he'll find out about it sooner or later."

"She'd like it to be lots later."

When all the gold was piled on the counter, Slocum and Little Britches sat on the hard depot bench waiting for Rensaleer.

Soon, a man in a rumpled suit and with a large mustache arrived clearing his throat. "What can I do for you?" He frowned at the canvas sacks. "This yours?"

"Yes."

"Do you have an assay report and a bonded weight?"

"I left four dead outlaws up north of here. I need this deposited in a Mexican bank for the owner."

"Who is that?"

"Lucia Valenta."

"Never heard of her. You will need an assayer's report." He shook his head.

"I want you to seal it and send it to the Bank of Sonora in Guaymas in the account of Lucia Valenta."

"I can't be responsible for any loss when I have not substantiated the value."

"Let's take the gold bars out, weigh them, and we can sack up the high-grade ore."

Rensaleer looked uncertain. "How did you get this gold anyway?"

"Mister, I've rode my ass off from the Sierra Madres to here to get it back from bandits."

The man frowned. "Did you bring in the bandits?"

"No. Some of 'em are dead up there. I left them for the buzzards. Two got away."

"There may have been a reward on them. The dead ones, I mean."

Slocum agreed. "I really only want this gold shipped."

"When we have the ore assayed, then we can establish a value."

This was not going to suit him. "Ship the damn bars to her bank. I'll figure out how to send her the ore."

"Whatever," Rensaleer said, "I will still need the bars weighed on an accurate scale. That's the only way I can be certain of any loss in the event of robbery. You may say it weighs more than it actually does. Thus, the claim would cost Wells Fargo more than they should have to bear."

"All right," Slocum said in surrender.

He went back outside, where Little Britches was with the horses, to talk to her. "This is going to be a bigger deal than I ever imagined. Why don't you take the stage to Dragoon Springs today? I'll close this shipping business out here and come on. The stage ride will be easier and you can get a jacal ready for us."

She perked up at his last words. "You won't have to run off?"

"I said get it ready for us. I can't stay forever. But I can for a while."

"You have a deal. When does the stage leave?"

"I'll find out—" His words were cut off by a shuttling locomotive's whistle.

She took the stage at ten o'clock and he kissed her good-bye, promising to be there as soon as he could.

"Don't be long," she said.

Parting with her stabbed his heart. Still, with Fine and St. John on the loose, he felt she'd be lots safer in Dragoon Springs than in New Mexico. Besides, the stage ride would be faster and more restful than the long hot ride on horseback.

He and Rensaleer completed their business by dark that evening—faster than Slocum expected, moving the gold on a buckboard under shotgun guard to the Columbus Assay office for careful weighing, and then to the local bank's safe.

Bored to death, he wondered how Little Britches was making it. He decided to take the gold ore with him after Wells Fargo's main office in San Francisco telegraphed Rensaleer that they would rather not ship it since its actual value was not verifiable.

At last, he dropped on the hotel bed, weary of the whole business, and before he fell asleep, he regretted sending her on ahead to Dragoon Springs. He'd be a few days getting to her—sell the extra horses, take two great packhorses to haul the ore . . .

He was short-loping the gray barb, grateful for the owner's "contribution" of the fine horse. With his Remington rifle under his right fender skirt, he felt rested as he led the bay horses he'd chosen for pack animals and the roan he figured would make Little Britches a good saddle horse later. He planned to make Lordsburg by late evening on his fresh horses.

It was past midnight when he arrived in Lordsburg, and the short main street was choked with a mob of people despite the late hour. He reined up the weary gray and asked a man standing by what was wrong.

" 'Paches struck a stage out by the playas—"

He bounded off the horse. "What happened?"

"They killed 'em all. Brought the bodies in an hour ago."

"Where are they?"

"Undertaker's, I guess. But from what they been saying, you won't want to see them."

"Mister, I'll pay you to watch my horses."

"Guess I can do that."

"Good." Slocum handed him his reins, and began making his way through the angry crowd listening to some orator rant about the "sorry army" that couldn't control the savages.

He slipped in the undertaker's door and removed his hat. He looked around, and a thin, drawn-faced man came out of the rear of the business. "May I help you?"

"The victims?" Slocum asked.

"They aren't suitable for viewing."

"I need to know about a certain young lady that might have been on board."

The man shook his head. "There was a young woman in her twenties, I would say—"

"I need to see if it is her."

The man's clear blue eyes studied Slocum for a moment. "I shall warn you, you may wish you'd never seen her like this."

Slocum waved him on, and followed him to the back of the building down a hall that reeked of death.

Four bodies were lined up on the table, each under a white shroud. When the man stepped to the second one in the row and pulled back the cloth, Slocum knew what he'd dreaded was true. Little Britches was dead.

20

The sun bore down hard on Slocum. Four days in the saddle with Captain Brown's company had them close to the Sierra Madres. Oppressive heat and afternoon rainstorms made the humidity unbearable. Ahead, the foothills promised some relief from the sweltering temperatures of the cactus and greasewood flats. The two Apache scouts were certain they had Kia-enta's tracks.

Slocum believed in their honesty and had stuck with Brown, who led one of of the several U.S. Army units crisscrossing northern Mexico in search of the lightning raid's leader. Kia-enta had left the dead strewn about from Globe, Arizona Territory, to the border.

At a midday break, Slocum sat on his butt in the lacy shade of a mesquite, hugging his knees and listening to Brown Boy, the younger of the two scouts, tell how Kia-enta drew the San Carlos Police away from the agency, then set fire to their haystacks and warehouse. The story was funny to the soldiers sitting about and the other scout. Little love was lost between the agency and the army. The army blamed the Apache problem on the agency's mismanagement since they'd wrenched the overseeing of the Apaches from the military.

Slocum agreed with that, too. The agency, like others,

answered to the Tucson Ring, who furnished whiskey and guns to the Apaches to keep the war going—and were making millions off the army as well.

Some upstart medicine man named Geronimo had paid two hundred dollars in gold Mexican coins apiece for new Winchester rifles. So Indians knew the value of money, and no longer poured it out on the ground to return it to the earth like earlier Indians did.

In the late afternoon, as Slocum and the soldiers rode skyward, a cool breeze off a nearby thunderstorm swept Slocum's whisker-stubbled face. He looked past the next juniper clump at the large billowing cloud in the southwest. More rain.

When he looked higher up the steep face of the mountain they rode up, the two scouts were coming on their short-legged ponies. He pushed the gray up beside Captain Brown and his sergeant.

Brown nodded to him. The scouts were coming, and that could mean word on Kia-enta.

Brown Boy slid his bay pony to a stop, and his narrowed eyes showed he meant business. "That sumbitch is only a short ways up the mountain in a camp."

"Who's with him?" Brown asked.

"Two white men. They make trade."

"Captain, let me and a few men go up there?" Slocum asked, feeling certain they were either whiskey peddlers or gunrunners. He wanted Kia-enta for murdering Little Britches.

Brown shared a quick look with his noncom.

The rugged sergeant nodded. "Campbell, Young, and Martin."

"All right, I know what this means to you," Brown said to Slocum. "But don't foolishly risk my men. It could be a trap."

"I won't."

The three troopers soon joined him, and the six, including the scouts, rode out, cat-hopping up the mountain on their horses. The two scouts were in the lead. Slocum knew the gathering thunderstorms might sweep in on them any moment. Towering cumulous cloud often rose to dazzling heights in moisture off the distant gulf, and then the rain, even hail sometimes, would pelt down. Up in the foothills, the air felt even cooler and caused goose flesh under Slocum's once-clammy shirt.

The first nearby bolt of lightning cracked like a rifle shot. It caused each rider to start and wonder for a millisecond if the battle had begun. Rain could make it impossible for Slocum to catch the Apaches in camp. Still, though with every lunge of his hard-breathing gray under him he knew his chances would be slim, hope rose inside him and fed his eagerness.

They reached a flat stretch of land, and rode through some stunted pines. He and the troopers followed the scouts, who made head signals to indicate changes of direction.

A whiff of wood smoke hit his nose. The Apache scouts had already dismounted. Campbell, a fair-skinned young man, was left in charge of their horses. With his Remington in his hands, Slocum hurried with the others uphill. Then he stopped beside the two Apaches as they looked down on a ranchero.

Women worked and children played around the wicki-ups beside the small stream. Several ponies grazed close by—four mules under packs were hitched in the midst of the camp. Obviously, some trading was going on. Slocum sighted through the rifle as the troopers spread out and bellied down on the ridge. He saw some hats—familiar ones, Freddie Fine's and Henry St. John's—but they were moving around and not in a clear enough position for a shot.

"Can you see them?" Brown Boy whispered to him.

"Not good enough to shoot them."

"Shoot the mules."

Slocum frowned. "Why?"

"They will soon know we are here and escape with them."

The youth had a point and knew Apaches. Killing the

mules would stop them from having whatever those two had brought up there to trade.

Slocum took out three cartridges from his vest pocket, set them close by, and then centered his sights on the closest mule. A shame was a shame. He squeezed off a shot, and the nearest pack animal crumpled. He recocked the rifle, flipped over the block, and extracted the shell from the smoking chamber. Another round in place, he drew down on the second mule, who acted skittish over the death of the first one.

Down he went. Unload and reload. Women were screaming as children ran about. He saw Freddie Fine standing with his eyes squinted and cursing him. Slocum drew a bead on him in the long tube and squeezed off the trigger. Gun smoke swept over his eyes.

The soldiers cheered, and Slocum decided his target was down. Rain struck his back as he reloaded. Large cold drops that felt like hail, though it had not formed yet. He tried to make one last shot—saw a spooked mule, took aim, and fired. It crumpled to the ground, and a curtain of hard downpour prevented him from seeing anything else.

Ear-shattering thunder, flashing lightning bolts, rain that drenched him to the skin—he knew the hostiles would use this opportunity to escape. Which way would they go?

"North or south?" He'd caught Brown Boy by the sleeve. For a second in the deluge, he wondered if the youth heard his shouting.

"South maybe?"

Slocum released him. He slid in slick mud, recovered on the run, and reached the horses. He was in the saddle. St. John and Kia-enta were still alive. He had no intention of either one escaping.

The rain stopped. The sun popped out. Slocum came out of a copse of pine and into the open, and could see one rider streaking south through a sagebrush clearing. He stopped, dismounted, jerking the Remington free, and cocked it. Water blurred the sight some, but he could see the rider flailing his mount. He pulled the trigger and it snapped—nothing.

His one good open shot—a dud.

Reload over his leg, then snap the block back in place. When Slocum found him again in his sight, Kia-enta was going up a steep bank, his pony obviously having to strain. Aim—fire.

The Apache's arms went skyward when the bullet struck him. His horse reared and fell over backward. They spilled on their backs down the hillside, both the stricken rider and his mount.

When Slocum looked away, Brown Boy was beside him.

"Where did St. John go?" Slocum asked.

The scout shook his head.

He wouldn't get far. Ready to cry, Slocum took the rifle by the barrel, strode to the nearest pine tree, and broke the stock against it. Then he tossed the barrel portion aside and dropped to his butt and wept in his hands. He should never have sent her on that stage.

21

The night in Agua Buena still held the day's hottest air. Slocum stood in the shadows, his clothing soaked in his own perspiration. He dried his gun hand on the side of his leg. Henry St. John was supposed to be coming.

At the sound of horses approaching, he nodded to himself. His man must at last be coming. No need to rush. Let them go into the cantina and he'd face him down in there.

Somehow, St. John had missed Slocum's traps up until this evening. He'd thought he'd had St. John up near the border, and like a fox the bandit had eluded him. The man's days were numbered. All Slocum could do was listen to the crickets chirp and regret not killing St. John the night he got the drop on him months earlier.

Before St. John killed Valenta, kidnapped Lucia—hell, Slocum's life was full of regrets and all of them came from stupid things he'd done.

The three riders dismounted and, talking in Spanish, went inside the cantina. One of them had to be St. John.

Slocum started across the street, then slipped between the cantina wall and another building. In the alley behind, he stepped carefully around the discarded broken bottles outside the rear door. It was made of old wood and had several cracks that he could spy through.

The light was dim and smoky. But he heard one voice ask in Spanish, "Where is he?"

They'd been forewarned—again.

He stepped back and slipped away. Let them fret. Whoever had informed them must be close to Slocum. He walked down the alley, and in few minutes was inside a dark jacal.

"Is that you?" a woman's sleepy voice asked.

"Yes." He toed off his boot.

"Did he come tonight?"

"It was a trap."

"Oh, who warned him?"

"Someone that knows too much about me."

She was sitting up on the bed. Starlight filtered in the glassless window. He could see her teardrop breasts, and they reminded him of her fiery hunger. She swept the thick black hair back from her face and shook her head. "I have no idea who it could be."

"I'll watch closer and catch them."

Undressed, he climbed in beside her. They kissed and she snuggled to him. With her firm breasts against his chest, her small hands groping him familiarly, they soon were one and he was hard at work. Then they exploded and fell apart on the bed, exhausted.

The next day, Slocum tried to become aware of any sign of betrayal. St. John had come and gone the night before. Slocum had missed him, certain that a trap had been planned for him in the cantina. So the cat-and-mouse game would continue.

No word of the bandit came for days. But Slocum felt certain he was still in the area. If St. John had left, then word would have come about that, too. For Slocum's part, all was working well. St. John would grow more reckless—considering Slocum had not taken his bait. Slocum needed some bait of his own.

Slocum did some riding and some scouting. He spoke to a few herders out with flocks, but they knew little about the outlaw. Then he found an old man who made jewelry. Seated cross-legged on the ground, he used a hammer and a fractured piece of railroad iron for an anvil.

"You have crosses for sale?" Slocum asked him when he dropped down from his horse.

"Ah, *sí, señor.* I have many." Under the lacy shade of the mesquite, his gentle face looked like soft leather as he nodded. He called out to his wife to bring out the samples.

A short woman in a brown dress held the choices out on a board.

"Gracias," Slocum said, and chose one he liked for the woman. "How much *dinero*?"

"Two pesos is a fair price."

Slocum nodded and squatted down close to the man. He put the money in his hand and the man smiled. *"Gracias."*

"There is a bandit lives in these hills," Slocum said.

"Ah, there are many bad men live around here."

"The one I want is St. John. Henry St. John."

The peel of the hammer striking the sliver on the anvil rang like a bell. The man did not look at him. "I know this man. He is very bad."

"Where does he live?"

"In the Tangue."

"Where is that?"

"A few kilometers east of here is a dry river. Once it ran, but there was an earthquake and it went dry. There is a deserted ranchero a few kilometers up that dry bed."

Slocum gave the man two more pesos and thanked him. The man nodded, but did not raise his head when Slocum stood up.

At the gray's side, Slocum checked the girth and swung up. "Thanks again."

The man only nodded.

In a short while, Slocum found the dry riverbed lined with the dead white trunks of cottonwoods. Kind of eerie-looking, he decided as he headed upstream. He could see the crude remains of an irrigation ditch on the once-productive land east of the dry river's course.

Short of the home place, he smelled smoke from a

cooking fire, dismounted, and used his field glasses to survey the place. Several old and young women worked around the buildings and the corrals. No sign of any man.

It was siesta time.

Slocum never knew for sure why he did it. He went back and mounted his gray. Then he rode him straight for the ranchero. Startled women saw him approach and blinked in shock. Hand to her mouth, one ran for the main house.

No doubt she'd wake St. John. The gray kept cutting down the distance. In a few minutes, a hatless St. John appeared in the doorway. He was strapping on his gun and his clumsiness showed as he fed the belt tongue into the buckle. Maybe he was so out of sorts because he'd just been asleep.

"You come a long ways to die?" St. John said.

"I was thinking the same thing of you." Slocum dismounted.

"This is my hacienda." St. John made a sweep with his hand to indicate the size.

"I didn't come to talk this time."

St. John nodded. "It was that girl, wasn't it?"

"It was the girl." Slocum punctuated the sentence with his .44. With the acrid smoke in his face, he watched the outlaw crumple. St. John dropped his unfired six-gun.

"You sumbitch . . ."

Slocum never bothered to answer him. The red blood on the man's chest told him enough. St. John would never rape another woman, never rob or kill anyone else.

Slocum mounted the gray and looked back at the wailing woman bent over him. *Don't cry for him. He wasn't worth it.* Then he turned the barb and rode away.

Damn Little Britches—he'd miss her.

22

It was past sundown when Slocum drew up at her jacal. The gray dropped his head in the dust and snorted wearily. The soft candlelight inside shone from the door on the dirt outside. A cur dog slunk over, wagging his tail and looking for affection, but carefully.

She rushed outside and looked for him in the starlight, then wrapped herself in the shawl against the cooling night as she ran to him. "You must leave. There are men here looking for you—bad men."

"Where are they?"

"In the cantina. One rides the spotted horse you told me about."

He hugged her and rested his cheek on top of her head. "The Abbott brothers. Deputies from Fort Scott, Kansas." He spoke it aloud more for his own benefit than hers. "You did good. I brought you a present."

From his pocket, he dug out the silver cross on the rawhide thong he'd strung it on and put it in her hands. It shone, and she nodded in approval.

Then, impulsively, she stood on her toes, swept off his hat, and made him bend down so she could put the cross over his head.

"You will need this more than I will—to escape these men."

He never argued, just kissed her hard, and she clung to him for a long moment. Then he released her and looked regretfully in the direction of the cantina. "I better go."

He reached back and adjusted the leather thong so the cross hung free over his chest under his shirt. With a nod for her, he went to his saddlebags and removed a buckskin pouch. He put the heavy leather gift in her hands.

"There is gold in there. Enough to care for you for some time."

"*Gracias, hombre.*"

Then he stepped in the stirrup, swung up, checked the gray, and nodded. "*Vayas con Dios,* my love."

"And you."

A week later, Slocum crossed through the rock *malpais* of Texas Canyon and in the midday sun studied the jacales and corrals of Dragoon Springs. He took a swig out of the neck of the whiskey bottle. He'd visited the Denning Methodist Church Cemetery, and the headstone he'd ordered for Little Britches's grave looked nice.

He wiped his hand over his whisker-bristled mouth, then took another swig. He had lots of forgetting to do. Lots of it.

Watch for

SLOCUM AND PEARL OF THE RIO GRANDE

356th novel in the exciting SLOCUM
series from Jove

Coming in October!